Croft's hands formed fists at his sides

"I'm not paying you to go off for illicit weekends," he accused.

"Illicit weekends!" Mercy echoed, incredulity in her eyes at his nerve. "It's your own urges you're talking about, not mine. It's you who needs an outlet, not me!"

"If at any time I ever feel the need to let my—urges, as you call them, get the better of me," Croft retaliated, "it might surprise you to know that you're not the only female of my acquaintance.

"D'you know, Mercy," he said with amusement, "we sound like an arguing married couple." Then, quietly, he said, "Fancy trying it?"

Mercy's eyes became huge as she sought comprehension. "You're suggesting...."

"I'm not suggesting anything your prim little soul could ever take exception to."

JESSICA STEELE

no quiet refuge

Harlequin Books

TORONTO • NEW YORK • LONDON
AMSTERDAM • PARIS • SYDNEY • HAMBURG
STOCKHOLM • ATHENS • TOKYO • MILAN

Harlequin Presents first edition August 1983
ISBN 0-373-10621-1

Original hardcover edition published in 1983
by Mills & Boon Limited

CHAPTER ONE

MERCY awoke, her eyes going automatically to her alarm clock. Then she remembered that this was the first day of her holiday, and the tip of her dainty pink tongue came out in a gesture to advise the offending instrument that, today, she was going to have a lie-in.

Not many minutes later, and frustratingly since any other morning she could easily have gone back to sleep—had not her conscience forced her out of bed and away to her job of school secretary—she discovered that this morning, she just did not feel sleepy.

Excitement, I expect, she thought, her mind already on that afternoon which would see her at Hilary Driver's family home on the outskirts of the village. Hilary had been her best friend at school, but correspondence between them had almost petered out. That was why it was such a delightful surprise to be invited to act as one of the bridesmaids at Hilary's wedding tomorrow.

Philip had been surprised too, she recalled, throwing back the covers and heading for the kitchen to make a cup of coffee. Though instead of standing at her kitchen table to drink it, as was usual on a weekday, she decided to have the luxury of a ten minute sit-down before she started her day. Her mind went back briefly to Philip Bailey, her fiancé although she wore no ring, agreeing with him as she had that the money could be put to better use for their future home.

Her eyes flicked down to the slender fingers of her bare left hand. Without envy the thought came that she'd like to bet Hilary was sporting a whacking great diamond. Hilary always had known what she wanted.

Five years ago when they had both been seventeen, Hilary had kicked her school hat into a hedge on their last day at school, and declared:

'That's school, that's Ravensmere. Coming to London with me, Mercy?'

It had been a terrific idea, Mercy had thought then. But her father had soon put a stop to that. 'You're going to secretarial college, young lady,' he had told her forcefully. 'Jack Driver can let his daughter do what he likes—but you're staying home.'

And she had stayed home. And for a whole year she had pined for the fabulous time Hilary wrote she was having. As Hilary had said, 'Nothing ever happens in Ravensmere.'

After her secretarial training Mercy had started work at the local school. Then, suddenly, she wasn't longing to join Hilary any more. For Philip, a teacher at the same school, had begun asking her out. She had known him to say 'Hello' to for years, but gradually, the more she got to know him, the more she began to value his worth.

They had started to date regularly, though at first she had been fearful her father might not like him. But her father too had seen that Philip was the right man for her. It was a joy to her that he had raised no objection to their becoming engaged.

Shortly after their engagement nearly a year ago, her father had acted upon what he had been talking of for years, telling her mother that with Mercy more or less settled, he was going to sell the house and that the two of them were going to Australia to live.

Philip had been a darling in those early days when she missed her mother acutely. And if there was a fly in Mercy's particular jar of ointment in that Philip had a mother too, a mother who must have off-loaded her share of human charity on to her son, for she had none, then Mercy tried hard to be as generous as Philip in his views of other people. She had never heard him say an unkind word about anyone.

Perhaps that was why it had come as something of a shock, when she told him Hilary had invited her to be her bridesmaid, to hear him ask:

'What does she want you for?'

Taken aback because he had never shown any of the aggression that was part and parcel of her father, she'd had to think for a moment, why indeed should the sophisticated Hilary want her for a bridesmaid.

'I'm—her friend,' she had brought out at last.

'But you haven't seen her for years.'

That was true enough. Hilary's last visit to Ravensmere had been a flying one, no time to look up old friends.

'That doesn't mean we're not friends still. We correspond . . .'

'Spasmodically,' Philip had put in, and she had been aghast that she and Philip, who never quarrelled, should suddenly appear to be in the middle of an argument.

'W-would you rather I didn't accept?' she questioned, quieting something in her that was objecting to her being so amenable.

But she was glad she had offered, even if she wasn't very sure about her offer. For Philip was suddenly her Philip again.

'Of course you must be her bridesmaid. Of course you must.' He squeezed her hand, and Mercy felt good again. Philip appeared to think Hilary was not quite the right sort of friend for her. But, as she had known, he was too generous, too kind and gentle to want to spoil things for her.

Though, strangely, she was troubled again to find later, after she had said goodnight to him, that a flicker of rebellion should make itself felt when she recalled his question of whether Hilary would be paying for her bridesmaid's dress. In truth, she hadn't given a thought to who would pay.

She pushed the hint of rebellion away. Philip was right, of course, it was silly to pay the earth for a dress she was only likely to wear once, when the money could be of far more use if put in their joint savings account. It wasn't as if they ever went places where a bridesmaid's dress, altered a little, could be worn again, was it?

Not feeling very comfortable with her thoughts, Mercy rinsed out her coffee mug, reflecting that she had better get a move on. She had promised herself she would do a few chores this morning that had been waiting for the holidays. She wouldn't be seeing Philip today, even though it was the first day of his holidays too. His mother had asked him to take her to see her sister in Leeds, and it would be too late when he got back for him to call—that was if he didn't want to have Miss Sefton twitching at her lace curtains. Though Miss Sefton liked Philip, she knew. It had been because of her liking for him that the security-conscious Miss Sefton had agreed to rent her the flat when her parents had sold up, she knew that too.

Still, she would see Philip at the wedding tomorrow. And anyhow, she had plans of her own for this afternoon. Hilary was driving down this morning. Luckily one of the other bridesmaids was Mercy's exact size, so it was to be hoped her own dress fitted.

Looking forward to seeing her friend again, at two o'clock Mercy locked the door of her flat, and was in the main street of the village before it came to her— she'd done it again! Although Philip had told her only the other day when he'd caught her at it, that Miss Sefton wouldn't approve of the habit she had of leaving her door key under the plant pot on her landing, that was exactly what she had done.

Guilt in her conscience was consoled by the memory

of the poor lighting on her landing, that part of the electricity included in her rent and a low wattage more than adequate in her landlady's opinion. The lighting was dimmer than dim there, she backed up her self-argument. It was so much easier to put her hand on the key knowing where she had placed it, than to stand there for five minutes rooting for the spare she kept in her handbag, which without fail proved elusive.

'Afternoon, Mercy.'

She looked up to see Mrs Jauncey, one of the dinner ladies from school, pedalling furiously by. 'Afternoon, Mrs Jauncey,' she called after her, having known the lady all her life.

In fact, she thought, as many such greetings were exchanged on her walk to the Drivers' home, there wasn't a face in the village that wasn't known to her, or her face known to them.

She could have gone to Hilary's in her car, she thought, but it was such a lovely day it seemed criminal not to walk. She nibbled at the inside of her lip as her thoughts followed on to Philip's tentative suggestion that she sell the car, and his saying it was an expense she didn't really need since he had a car she could use.

It was common sense, she could see that, and the money from the sale would boost their savings a little, but the small saloon model that had been her father's was the one she had learned to drive on, and she didn't want to part with it. Though whether it was because she was sentimentally attached to it, or whether it was because to have her own car gave her a feeling of independence, she wasn't sure.

Not happy that it might be the latter, not happy that she should want to feel independent from Philip in any way, her thoughts on the matter were sent on their way when Mrs Vialls, chief among the village's gossip-mongers, sailed into view.

She wished then that she had decided to go by car

after all. It was going to take all of ten minutes to get by Mrs Vialls. She hurried her step, trying to make it look as though her journey was urgent.

'No Philip Bailey today?' enquired Mrs Vialls, doing away with a greeting, her bulk blocking the path as Mercy, her steps slowing, made to sidle round.

'Not today,' she smiled. Mrs Vialls was a friend of Philip's mother. If Mercy offended her, Philip would hear all about it *ad infinitum* from Mrs Bailey.

'I thought I saw him taking his mother out in the car?'

'They've gone to Leeds for the day.'

'Oh yes, I remember now,' said Mrs Vialls, who had the memory of an elephant and never forgot a snippet. 'Such a long drive to do in one day, but I expect you'll want him there at the wedding tomorrow.' Mercy kept her smile in place at the implication that she was making Philip break his neck to get back. 'He's such a nice boy,' the stout lady added when no rise was forthcoming.

Mrs Vialls, Mercy thought, looked to be nearing sixty, so perhaps Philip, at thirty-two, did seem to be a nice boy to her. 'Yes, he is,' she agreed, and edged to the side in a move to try and get away.

'Have you set your wedding day yet?' asked the inquisitor, her third chin wobbling.

'Next year some time,' said Mercy, able to give the information freely since Philip had acquainted his mother with the news.

'You'll be off to the Drivers' now, I expect,' said Mrs Vialls, having already filed away for future use what she had just learned. 'I saw that Hilary arrive just before lunch.'

'I must go, I'm going to be la . . .'

'Leaving it a bit fine, isn't she,' interrupted the local Clarion, opining, 'She should have been down here before this—leaving her parents to cope with everything. Her poor mother has been run off her feet.'

'I must . . .'

'There'll be no time for a church rehearsal. I saw the vicar only yesterday, and he was telling me . . .'

It was Mercy's turn to interrupt. 'You'll have to excuse me, Mrs Vialls,' she said, for Philip's sake forcing another smile. She made it round her, and glanced at her watch without noticing the time. 'I'm already ten minutes late.'

She let out a sigh of relief as she escaped past the gossipy woman. And by the time she had reached her destination, she had all but forgotten the encounter, resigned as she was to the fact that village life was like that. Everyone knew everyone else; stopping for a gossip was all part of it. And if there were some members of the community who invented what they did not know, then it was probably the same in any area.

Justin Driver, Hilary's sixteen-year-old brother and needing someone to give him a clip round the ear in Mercy's opinion, was the one who opened the door to her.

'Light of my life!' he gasped, clutching his heart and staggering back as he saw her standing there.

'Hello, Justin,' she answered, not prepared to give him the yard he would take if she gave him an inch. 'I hear Hilary has arrived.'

'Come in and join the madhouse,' he invited, and promptly as she crossed the threshold, 'Are you still going out with Old Bailey?'

'Justin,' said Mercy warningly.

'Wouldn't his mother let him out?' he asked, unabashed, unrepentant when he could see she was far from amused. 'Forgive me,' he said, his face adopting a solemn mask, 'but it's hard to take that you love another,' and, unable to keep his impudence down, 'and *what* another!'

Wanting to be that donor of a thick ear herself,

Mercy controlled the urge. 'I shall be glad, Justin Driver, when you grow up,' she said instead.

But the instant she saw the warm red colour come up beneath his skin at her attempt to cut him down to size, she was regretting her words. He was too cocky by half, but he obviously thought he was already grown up, and found her words far more searing than she had meant them to be.

But before she could make any effort to salve his damaged pride—much as his remarks about Philip had earned him a set-down—the door of the drawing room opened, and there stood Hilary, looking more poised and elegant than ever.

'Darling! How simply divine to see you!' Hilary exclaimed. And Mercy was at once aware what a lot of water had gone under the bridge since she and this sophisticate had been best friends.

But half an hour later up in Hilary's old room, Hilary's affected front had in some part been disposed of, and she was some way nearer to being an old friend as Mercy stood for inspection in her brides-maid's dress.

'The fit's perfect,' pronounced Hilary, walking round her and surveying with a sharp eye the palest of green chiffon that had been transformed by some magical dressmaker into a high-necked, long-sleeved dress. 'In fact,' said her friend, 'you look great.'

Mercy couldn't help but admire herself too. 'Great' was perhaps an overstatement, but she did look good in the dress, the style suited to her short dark hair with its tendency to curl.

'It's a beautiful dress,' she agreed. 'I was rather afraid . . .' She stopped, realising she had been about to be tactless. Then discovered that her friend knew what she had been about to say anyway.

'You were afraid the neck line might be more décolleté than décolleté?'

'Well,' Mercy said lamely, 'You're so much more with it in London, aren't you?'

'I did think of something low and stunning to make the villagers' eyes pop out,' Hilary said with a grin of candour that went a long way to close the gap of the five years since she had left Ravensmere. 'But with Giles being the quiet sort, I thought better of it.'

Mercy was interested in Giles. So far very little had been said about him. She owned some surprise though that he should be 'the quiet sort'. For whenever Hilary had remembered to write, it was never without including a mention of some wild party or other she had been to.

'He—likes a quiet life?' she asked, and saw Hilary's face go pensive momentarily before her smile came out as she nodded, and said:

'I shall have to work on him.' And her smile becoming a grin again, 'Though since it took me all my time to get him to agree to a big wedding, I reckon I shall have my work cut out.'

'Giles would have preferred a quiet wedding?'

'You bet,' confirmed Hilary. 'He hates fuss of any sort. I shall be on pins tomorrow in case he funks it and doesn't turn up.'

Mercy could see from her expression that she didn't think there was much likelihood of that. 'No way,' she said.

'No, you're right. Though he'd have grabbed at the idea of getting married without all the fuss, if I had consented,' she said, going on to tell Mercy how he was going to hate having all eyes on him, and relating how he had nearly died of embarrassment when at a party she had dragged him to, some girl had made an outrageous scene and that while everyone else seemed to be enjoying it, she had taken one look at Giles and had quickly got him out of there.

'But he wasn't at the centre of the scene, was he?'

questioned Mercy, starting to like Giles although she had never met him. She hated scenes too.

'He'd have had heart failure on the spot if he had been,' Hilary replied, so much conviction in her voice that Mercy was prompted to ask quickly:

'There's nothing wrong with his heart, is here?' Though she managed to hold down the impulse to ask how old Giles was.

'Not a thing, save he says he has given it to me,' said Hilary openly. More openly than Mercy would have done; Philip never went in for such talk, but if he had she would have regarded it as private. 'And to save you having a shock tomorrow, he's forty-four,' Hilary went on, answering Mercy's unvoiced question, 'thinning on top, has enough money to keep me in comfort for the rest of my life, and . . .'

'And you love him,' put in Mercy with a gentle smile.

'You haven't changed, still the same romantic soul you always were,' Hilary commented, then was thoughtful for a moment, before she said, 'And yes, I love him. I didn't at first, I have to admit it—though only to you. At first all I could see was his gold-lined wallet.'

Mercy's eyes shot wide at this revelation that her friend's initial interest was in his bank balance. Then Hilary was telling her that the more she learned of Giles, the more she became attracted to him, and Mercy promptly forgot what she had said before as tomorrow's bride went on:

'I found myself doing things just to please him. A change from thinking only of myself,' she said ruefully. 'Oh, I'm not saying I don't still like a good time, but— it's different this time.'

'You've been in love before?'

'Half a dozen times, but not like this. When Giles asked me to marry him, I couldn't get an answer out fast enough in case he changed his mind.'

'I'd better get out of this dress,' said Mercy, Hilary's romantic secrets having reminded her that Philip hadn't exactly proposed to her—they had just somehow drifted from talk of 'We'll do this or that' to talk of 'We'll do this when we're married'. She found all this talk of romance faintly unsettling.

With Hilary's help, she got out of her long dress and the long slip that went with it, both of them taking more time out to admire the pale green creation as it hung on its hanger against the wardrobe door.

'It's right for you,' said Hilary. 'Just as you're exactly right to be one of my bridesmaids.'

There was something in the way she said that that suggested that somewhere along the way she hadn't been too certain.

'You sound as though you weren't very sure until this moment?'

'Bridal nerves, I expect,' was the easy reply, and in honest confession, just like the old days, 'There were so many girls I could have asked to be my third bridesmaid. All like me, knowing it all and sharp with it. My chief bridesmaid is one such, so is Pamela, the second bridesmaid.' Suddenly her grin was wide and impish, the way it had been at seventeen. 'You're my concession to Giles,' she said. 'He'll just love you with your home-spun look, your minimum of make-up and your home-set hair.'

'I have an appointment at the hairdresser's tomorrow morning,' said Mercy, not quite sure how she felt about being called home-spun.

'Well, don't for goodness' sake let them spoil it. I want Giles to see I do have some friends who weren't born without natural simplicity.'

Mercy wasn't sure she liked that much either. Though she was begining to warm to Giles more and more. It sounded very much as though he went in for the peaceful life—which made her wonder how Hilary would fare when married, since she had spoken of still liking a good time.

'You're—sure?' she ventured to ask, marriage in her view being sacred, and not to be undertaken lightly.

'About Giles and me, you mean? Yes,' she said, 'Yes, I'm sure.' And, looking as happy as any girl about to be married should look, she reminded her, 'Didn't I tell you I'd had a good look round before I fell permanently in love?' Then, cutting short any more questions Mercy might find to ask, she suddenly switched the conversation without going into detail of what she had been up to since she had left Ravensmere. 'What about you?'

'Me!' Mercy exclaimed, knowing she was the least important person in the weekend's activities. 'What about me?'

'Well, are you still engaged to that Philip Bailey for one?' she asked with a swift look at Mercy's ringless hands.

'Yes, I am,' said Mercy a shade coolly, not liking the way Hilary had referred to Philip.

'Oh, don't get huffy, there's a dear. I sent your invitation to include a partner, but I . . .' She broke off, her shrewd blue eyes softening, 'It's only you I'm thinking of. I've told you I looked around a bit before I settled for Giles. It just occurred to me that it wouldn't hurt you to look around a bit too before you commit yourself.'

'I am committed.' Momentarily she thought, 'Hilary's only thinking of me, after all.' Then she saw from that knowing look in Hilary's eyes that she had misunderstood.

'You don't have to marry the first man you go to bed with,' the bride advised, obviously thinking that that was what Mercy had meant by saying she was committed. 'I mean, Philip Bailey might be good in bed—' she didn't quite manage to cover her look that said it would be a surprise to her if he was—'but so are a good many other men.'

Aware that they were embarking on a subject of which she had very little knowledge, though clearly that was not the case with Hilary, Mercy made haste to terminate the conversation.

'I love him, Hilary.'

She then received her friend's long look before, shelving what she had been going to say, Hilary dropped the subject with, 'Well, he's your choice.' She seemed tempted to say more, but changed her mind as a car could be heard coming up the drive. 'Come on, let's go down—the parents are back.'

With only herself for company that night, Mercy had a lot of time in which to go over the couple of hours she had spent in the Drivers' home. And by the time she took herself off to bed, it was to be oddly worried, that, because of those few hours spent with Hilary, she was feeling a tinge dissatisfied with her lot.

It was a startling realisation, especially since she knew positively that she wasn't at all envious of Hilary. She lay sleepless for an age, telling herself she was happy in Ravensmere, happy here with Philip for goodness' sake.

She turned over in bed, her mind going to that conversation she had ended when it had come round to Philip and whether or not he was good in bed. She knew exactly why she had ended that particular conversation, of course. She could never have confessed that she and Philip had never been to bed together. Experienced in such matters as Hilary undoubtedly was, Mercy knew she would still have been laughing had she told her that while she wouldn't have minded a bit more—well, passion, she supposed—Philip, dear, gentle Philip, had told her he wanted them both to be chaste when they stood before the minister.

The next morning Mercy found it an unaccustomed

treat to sit in the one-room village hairdressing salon and to leave the shampooing in the capable hands of Betty Mason, otherwise known as Elizabeth Coiffures.

Betty brought her head up from the wash-basin and wrapped a warm towel around her head, as, rushed off her feet, she went to comb out Mrs Holmes, the president of the W.I., while her young assistant went to bring Mrs Tandy, the Drivers' cleaning lady, complete with a head full of pink plastic, out from under the drier.

All three were going to the wedding, though Mercy was soon to learn, in a muttered aside, that Mrs Tandy had work to do before she went to the church to see her employer's daughter married.

'I hope she won't be long,' she muttered with a dark glance in Betty's direction. 'I promised Mrs Driver I'd go along there and give a hand as soon I could.'

'I don't expect she will be,' Mercy murmured consolingly.

'You'll have plenty of time to get everything organised,' boomed Mrs Holmes from the other side of Mercy (nothing wrong with her hearing). 'The wedding isn't until four o'clock.'

'A daft time of day to get married, if you ask me,' stated Mrs Tandy. 'If they'd had it earlier all those hordes of relatives coming from far and wide could have gone straight to church and said their "Hello's" afterwards.'

'It's probably because so many people are coming from away,' placated Mrs Holmes, 'that the wedding has been arranged for that time—to enable everybody to get here.'

'More likely because Madam Hilary wants to enjoy being queen bee at the party afterwards,' sniffed Mrs Tandy.

'It will be a lovely party, I'm sure,' said Mercy, thinking it about time she said something to smooth over what could break out into an argument, since Mrs Holmes seemed to be ruffling Mrs Tandy's feathers. 'Hilary did come home specially to get married, after all, when she could just as easily have got married in London.'

She jumped in again when Mrs Tandy looked about to open her mouth to say it was no more than Hilary should have done.

'Because we're miles away from any large airport, it will be too late after the wedding for them to fly off on their honeymoon. I'm sure Hilary thought how nice it would be for us all to enjoy an extended reception afterwards.'

Mrs Tandy didn't look convinced, but just then the girl assistant came to unwind her very fine hair from its mound of pink, and distracted her attention by yanking at one roller that had got tangled up.

'Ouch! That hurt,' she cried.

'Sorry, Mrs Tandy,' replied the young Christine, though she didn't really look it.

'See you later,' said Mrs Holmes over the top of Mrs Tandy telling Christine threateningly what she was going to do to that young Justin if he started with his tricks today.

Mercy was pleased with Betty's efforts with the blow dryer, though as she stepped outside and saw the overcast sky, she considered that one short sharp shower would probably have her hair looking much the way it had looked before Betty had got busy.

Excitement was with her as she drove the same route her feet had taken yesterday. She had returned to her flat after her visit to the hairdresser's, planning to have a bite to eat since she wasn't due at the Drivers' until two. But with that excitement in her she didn't feel hungry, and decided she would have calmed down when the buffet got under way afterwards, and she would eat then. She hadn't eaten breakfast either, she recalled as she parked her car on the drive among the many models later than hers outside Hilary's house.

The front door stood open. Mercy went in, and couldn't but muse, as people of all shapes and sizes tripped in and out of downstairs rooms, talk and laughter filling the place, that if Justin had thought the place like a madhouse yesterday, what then would he think it was like today.

'Have you eaten, Mercy?' Hilary's mother came up to her looking harassed, while doing her best to look serene.

'Yes, thank you, Mrs Driver,' she fibbed. 'Can I do anything to help?'

'No, dear, no. Everything is under control,' answered that lady, her ability to lie matching Mercy's. 'The girls are all upstairs waiting for you to join them.'

Hilary did not look a scrap nervous, Mercy thought, when she went into her bedroom and saw her wrapped in a housecoat and holding court with two of the most sophisticated young women she had ever seen. The blood-red finger nails of all three of them flattened her shiny pink-tinted clear nail polish into obscurity. And she was soon to discover that Hilary had donned the same mantle of sophistication with which she had greeted her yesterday.

'Darling,' she crooned. 'Come and say hello to my two dearest friends, Pamela and Georgiana.'

Traditionally, Hilary was late, though not more than five minutes. But although it was summer, the afternoon had turned wintry, which didn't suit Pamela and Georgiana at all as they protested at some length in loud ultra-refined voices about the cold and their thin dresses.

When Hilary arrived Mercy lined up beside Pamela to go down the aisle, Georgiana as chief bridesmaid following directly behind Hilary and her father. The organ swelled and there was movement inside as everyone stood up. And then the journey to the altar began.

It was a lovely church, the same church in which she and Philip would next year exchange their vows, Mercy thought, as she followed in the wake of the three in front. Memory of Philip set her eyes searching the left-hand pews to catch a glimpse of him.

The back pews were crowded with villagers, she saw as the procession turned round the curve at the back of the church. Down the centre aisle they moved with all eyes on the bride. Mercy felt good inside that Hilary, looking so beautiful, should have so many friends there to wish her well, to look at her with that warm look one reserved for brides.

Then, with everyone looking at Hilary, suddenly Mercy was jolted out of her happy thoughts. For, still searching for a glimpse of Philip, her eyes met, and held full on, a pair of eyes that were paying not the smallest attention to the bride!

Unable to look away, she was fixed by grey eyes that were hard, certainly no warmth in them, and she was shocked by the expression on the man's face that told her that in his view, the bride was beneath his notice.

Those hard eyes were looking steadily back at her, taking in her alone in her pale green dress and her widening brown eyes as the thought came to her; surely this tall fair-haired man had little interest in the proceedings? Yet, since he was here, he must have been invited—must have accepted that invitation!

Any idea of looking for Philip went out of her head as with a feeling akin to relief she passed by the man. He was nothing to do with her, she told herself. So why should she feel that chill of alarm run up her spine?

Then she saw Giles and his best man waiting for them, and as the marriage service began she put all her powers of concentration on trying to forget all about the man who just by looking at her had made her feel a flutter of panic. But she found it was not easy.

Why had he been looking at her anyway? He looked as sophisticated as any of the set Hilary ran around with. She would have thought, had his thoughts been bridesmaid-oriented, that the stylish Pamela or Georgiana would be more in his line.

Determinedly, she turned her mind away from him, telling herself she had been alarmed for nothing. It was just that he was a typically wordly-wise male and that weddings bored him. It was only that it appeared she had caught his attention, but it must have been a trick of the light, no more. Why, she'd wager that if it wasn't for the fact that she was one of the three girls dressed in long pale green, he wouldn't so much as remember her at the reception.

Giles looks a nice man, she thought, disturbed to find it wasn't so easy to eject the hard-eyed man from her thoughts. Hilary had said Giles was forty-four. Mercy concentrated on Giles, but only to discover that her wayward mind had gone on to wondering how old the grey-eyed man was. Around thirty-five, she decided, easily remembering the broad-shouldered look of him in his dark lounge suit. He looked an athletic sort, her recalcitrant mind went on. He . . .

She turned her thoughts away. And as Hilary began to give her responses, at last, unexpected moisture coming to Mercy's eyes, she finally forgot about the man who had managed to disturb her so.

Hilary seemed more protective of Giles than the other way around when they all went into the vestry. And it was then that Mercy knew that if her friend had had to look around a little until she had found the one man she could truly love, then she had, at last, found him.

Everyone was again standing when they made the return trip up the aisle, and already a less formal atmosphere prevailed. Happiness was again with Mercy as she fell into step, unconscious of the dewy-eyed look she wore at the lovely feeling she had inside that this was Hilary's happiest hour.

An elderly uncle of Giles' was escorting her to the church door, and she was to be glad that his quick reflexes belied his years. For when she came to where the hard-eyed man had been standing, having no intention of looking his way, indeed, not so much as thinking about him, Mercy's eyes turned in his direction.

And there he was again, looking fully at her and nowhere else, one corner of his mouth quirking ever so slightly when she stumbled and the uncle's loose hold on her arm tightened.

Hot colour darted to her cheeks. 'Thank you,' she gasped, glad to see the church doors were wide, cool air rushing in as they turned the bend.

'Saving on lighting, I should think,' excused the uncle, as though he wasn't surprised that anyone should stumble in the shadowed interior.

Outside the church she stood chatting to some of the village people while the main photographs were being taken. But it wasn't until one of them remarked, 'Where's Philip?' that it came to her, and with a start of guilt, that she had forgotten all about him when coming from the vestry.

'He's here somewhere,' she said confidently, but had no time to look around, for just then she heard the photographer calling for the bridesmaids.

The photography seemed to go on for the next half hour. And it was during this time, when not called to be in the picture, that Mercy looked about for Philip, though she was careful at the same time not to let her eyes stray in the direction of the grey-eyed man, for she knew quite well where he was. He was standing a little apart from everyone else, just as though, she thought, he wanted to dissociate himself from any of the proceedings.

She was beginning to wonder why he had come, since he didn't look at all pleased to be there. She even wondered briefly if he was one of the men Hilary had been in love with before she had found her true love in Giles. She rejected that idea. He didn't look like anybody's idea of unrequited love.

The bride and groom were ready to lead the way to the reception, everyone shivering with cold from standing about for so long, when all at once, looking at Hilary, Mercy saw she looked suddenly more white than pale.

It's the cold, I expect, she thought. And then had her attention drawn to where Mrs Tandy, despite her sour comment about 'Madam Hilary' at the hairdresser's, was opening a box of confetti ready to shower the happy couple.

Then all at once her attention was brought back to Hilary. For the bride had halted on her way to the waiting Rolls. And there was that in her voice as she spoke, that struck a chord of remembrance in Mercy. Her friend was sounding exactly the way she used to when trying to keep the lid down on threatening panic, in danger of being found in some disgraceful misdemeanour!

'I should like to be photographed with each of my bridesmaids in turn,' Hilary announced with a smile at Giles, who was looking more than eager to step out of the limelight and let the bridesmaids take over. 'It will be nice to have in our wedding album, won't it, darling?'

Mercy put from her the thought that Hilary was in any way panicking over something. Her friend had grown far too cool and poised to let any trivial upset mar this day of all days, she thought. And she watched as first Georgiana, and then Pamela, posed with the bride. She hadn't seen Philip yet, she reflected while she waited, and there had been ample time for him to seek her out.

Then it was her turn to go and stand beside Hilary. And as dutifully she stepped forward, Philip again went from her mind, because, close up, she could see that things were far from well with her old school friend.

'What's wrong?' she asked, knowing for sure now that something very definitely was. Although Hilary's mouth was smiling, it was impossible for anyone who knew her well not to notice that her blue eyes were not smiling, that those blue eyes were looking positively haunted!

'Smile,' was the answer she received. 'Smile, and for heaven's sake help me.'

She sounded desperate! 'Help you with what?' Mercy queried, doing what she could to hide the trepidation growing in her.

'Do you see that man over there by the yew tree? The one Georgiana has just sidled up to.'

Mercy had no need to look, but did. He wasn't looking at Georgiana, who didn't appear to be having any luck if she was trying to make an impression, he was looking straight at her, Mercy!

'Yes, I see him,' she muttered, not as expert as Hilary in smiling while carrying on an undercover conversation, but doing her best. 'Who is he—an old flame?' She asked the question even though it didn't make sense. Was Hilary likely to ask an old flame to her wedding if he had the power to make her look frightened to death?

'No, nothing like that,' came the muttered reply, and in a louder voice to the photographer, 'I'm sorry, I moved. Could you take that again?' She smiled a practised smile, then answered Mercy's other question: 'His name is Croft Latimer,' but volunteered nothing more about him.

'But . . .' said Mercy, having got the man's name, but still perplexed.

'There's no time to explain now,' Hilary said, that note of panic there in her voice again. 'Just listen and do as I tell you. Croft Latimer's here to make trouble, I know he is. If you don't do as I ask he'll make the biggest scene of all time. He'll hurt Giles—and Giles— Giles will never forgive me.'

CHAPTER TWO

With so much going on, everyone crowding round throwing confetti as Hilary and Giles attempted to step into the Rolls, Mercy found the moment she needed to escape, to be by herself.

Unnoticed she slipped into the church porch and was still thunderstruck that she had responded to the panic in Hilary's voice, and had promised she would keep *that* man, now known as Croft Latimer, out of Giles' way.

As Hilary had said, there had been no time for explanations, but already Mercy was regretting having given her promise. Even without ever having spoken to that hard-eyed individual, she just knew she was wholly unequipped to deal with a man like that.

She had known it as she had protested that her friend should make her request to Georgiana or Pamela. Had known with certainty that the task was more in their line than hers. But the horrified look in Hilary's eyes at her suggestion had shown that it had to be Mercy.

'For pity's sake,' Hilary had whispered hoarsely, 'don't let *them* know. They'd blab it all over London that I was reduced to a panicking country hick when he turned up—I'd be a laughing-stock.' And while still managing a smile for the cameraman, she had gripped her arm. 'Promise me you'll do it. Promise me. I implore you, Mercy, not to let me down.'

What could she say? 'All right,' she'd heard herself promise.

And now she had had all of five minutes by herself, and she was still wishing Hilary had asked one of her other bridesmaids to do it.

Without any trouble she recalled the way Croft

Latimer had only just managed to keep from looking bored when Georgiana had tried to hold his attention. And she knew then that, promise or no promise, short of knocking him on the head with something and trussing him up somewhere, she stood as little chance of keeping him away from Giles as of flying.

Her insides churning at the knowledge that she was going to have to make some attempt anyway, she became aware that the babble of voices had ceased. She moved from the porch and inwardly groaned to see that while she had been taken up with her thoughts, everyone had gone.

Oh no, she thought, her feet moving quickly down through the churchyard, already she had fallen down on her assignment! Croft Latimer could even now be arriving at the reception! Right at this moment he could be making that terrible scene that Hilary was dreading.

Mercy picked up her feet, her hand clutching at her dress whose hemline would have prevented her from moving with any speed. Her mind was fixed on stopping the first car she saw and grabbing a lift to Hilary's home as she raced towards the church gate.

But as she hurried through the gate, her feet came to an abrupt and sudden stop. Her heart then started to send out a rapid beat that could not be put down entirely to her sprint.

For there, parked where she was sure it had not been before, was a gleaming black Mercedes. Mercedes were rarely seen around the village, but that fact was not responsible for her hasty heart-beat either. That responsibility lay in the fact that a man was leaning back against the car. A tall, broad-shouldered man. A man with grey eyes. Eyes that were looking directly into her wide, amazed brown eyes. So Croft Latimer had not yet reached the wedding reception. He was right there, saying nothing—apparently waiting for her to get her breath back, waiting for her to speak first.

She gulped down her panic; there was no time then for her to get her thoughts into any sort of order. All she had time for was to recall that if she didn't do something about it, then her friend Hilary—her best friend—stood to have her marriage ruined before it so much as got started.

Hoping to find a smile that would conceal her inner quailing, she closed the small gap between church gate and car, and went to address the man who, so far, had not moved.

'How glad I am to see you,' she smiled. 'It would appear that I'm stranded.'

At the sound of her voice he straightened up, and Mercy's insides did a quick flip as she thought that if his eyes glazed over with that near-to-bored look he had given Georgiana, she just didn't know how she was going to manage to keep her smile in place. Then she heard his voice, cultured, even, though what he said was of no help at all, as coolly he replied:

'So it would.'

Her smile threatening to founder, she made gallant efforts to pull herself together. 'Since you're going to the reception too, Mr Latimer,' she said, and immediately wanted the ground to open up at her slip— she hadn't yet been introduced to him! She forced herself to go on, 'Er, could I beg a lift with you?' And she started to dislike him intensely because he had made her ask for a lift when he could just as easily have offered.

'You have the advantage of me,' he said. And when she hadn't a clue what he was talking about, 'Miss . . .' he hinted.

'Mercy Yeomans,' she obliged instantly, feeling herself colour at the thought that he must think she was interested in him and had asked Hilary his name.

She was still uncertain if she was going to have to cadge a lift from any passing mobile villager, when his warm right hand came out to cover her freezing cold one. But with the formal handshake completed, Croft Latimer did not immediately let go his hold, but kept her hand in his clasp as he escorted her round to the passenger's side of his car.

'You hands are like ice,' he commented. 'I think we'd better get you somewhere warm, don't you, Mercy?'

She smiled and hoped she looked calm. Hoped he had no idea how agitated she felt as he got his long length inside the car and pulled away.

'You'll have to direct me,' he remarked, which gave her an opening to ask:

'You've never been to Hilary's home before?'

Her answer was silence. But since a tractor in front was turning right and seemed to be what he was concentrating on, she hoped it was that and not because the mention of Hilary's name had turned him sour on her.

Looming large in the forefront of Mercy's mind was her unwanted reponsibility. She had to somehow or other keep this man occupied until the evening was safely over. Not that her duty would extend past the reception, but it was up to her to keep him pleasant until it was over.

'You don't come from around this way, Mr Latimer?' she made herself ask. Oh dear, there were hours yet to go before she could even begin to think 'mission accomplished'—if she didn't run out of steam, as she was afraid she might before many more minutes were up.

'Croft,' he replied, thus giving her permission to use his first name, the only information he did give her.

With a rush of irritation, since even the most innocent of questions she put to him went unanswered, Mercy saw she didn't stand a snowball in hell's chance of getting through until the reception ended without blowing up if he carried on like this. In her view there were quite a few questions that wanted answering by him *and* Hilary. It just wasn't fair to throw her in at the deep end and leave her to sink or swim.

Then she remembered the panic in Hilary. Remembered too how in church she had thought what a nice person Giles looked. And when for herself she would have taken no further trouble with him, it struck her that if she was to live with her conscience afterwards, she would just have to keep that promise to Hilary—as far, that was, as Croft Latimer would allow her to.

'Turn right here,' she told him, and having broken her silence, 'Do you know any of Hilary's family? I'll introduce you round if . . .'

The sudden coldness emanating from him made her break off, aware that he was objecting—but to what? Was he vexed at the way she was assuming he would stay by her side once they had reached Hilary's house? She soon discovered a strange relief shooting through her, that it was not her proposed annexation of him that he was objecting to.

'I'd rather you didn't do any introducing,' he said smoothly.

From which she could only conclude that the only person he was in any way interested in talking to, had to be Giles! It was all the confirmation she needed that Hilary had been right in thinking he was there only to make a scene.

Relief ebbed as panic started inside Mercy. Like Giles she didn't like scenes either, but she knew right then that there was one almighty scene brewing. Just as she knew then exactly why Croft Latimer had made sure he was the last to leave the place where the marriage ceremony had been performed.

He had deliberately stayed behind, she comprehended, so that when he did make it to the reception, everyone, bride, groom, and all the guests, would be assembled;

what he had to say would be overheard by every one of them!

He hadn't noticed that she hadn't gone with the other bridesmaids, had missed seeing that she had been left behind at the church. Not that one guest less would have made any difference to what he had to say, she thought, wondering what chance she'd got of deflecting him from his purpose if she pleaded with him not to do anything to spoil her friend's wedding day.

'Oh, what a pity,' she said, grasping at speech in an attempt to overcome her rising alarm. 'It's come on to rain.'

'It's been promising all day,' Croft Latimer replied, that word 'promising' not needing to be said to remind her of her promise made to Hilary with no time to think about it first.

'I hope the weather doesn't spoil Hilary's day,' she said in a rush. 'Nothing should be allowed to spoil a bride's wedding day, should it?'

She prayed he would take the hint, but turning her eyes to him she saw his face was set in harsh lines, and she knew then that her prayers were going to go unanswered. And she was gabbling then, the Drivers' home only two minutes away.

'Hilary is your friend too, as well as mine, you wouldn't want . . .'

'Did I say she was a friend?'

'But—she must be—must have been once,' Mercy blurted out—no time now to choose her words. 'You were on the bride's side of the church.'

That of course told him she had seen him, been aware of him, she thought, a fact she would have concealed if she hadn't been so anxious about Hilary, about how Hilary's parents were going to feel, to say nothing of how wretched this man apparently had the power to make poor Giles feel.

Then suddenly, Croft Latimer's face came out of its

stern lines. And although he wasn't exactly smiling, there was a shade more warmth in him when he said:

'I noticed you too,' adding, 'not unnaturally.'

She gathered from that 'not unnaturally' that he must mean because she had been not far behind the bride, which had been where everyone else was looking. But she was shaken as she directed him into the gates of the Drivers' large house, to hear him say:

'Far from being a friend of your friend. I have only ever seen her once in my life.'

She was still chewing on that when he stopped the car and came round to her door, then hurried her inside the house out of the downpour.

And again there was no time for her to think for very long. Because Hilary and Giles were just then receiving the last of their guests, accepting their congratulations, and before she knew it, it was her turn and Croft Latimer's turn. This was the moment when she had to go into action and make any conversation he had with Giles, the briefest on record.

'Ah, Mercy,' said Hilary, her smile forced, fear only in her eyes as they shifted from her and on to Croft Latimer. 'We were wondering where you had got to.' And speedily, before Croft could say a word, 'This is my very dear friend Mercy, Giles.'

Whether Croft shook hands with either of them, Mercy was too agitated to notice. She had read correctly the terrified fear Hilary was trying to hide, and wasted not a second before she acted. Her arm in its pale green sleeve was through Croft Latimer's as, before she knew it, she had hooked herself onto him. She appeared not to notice his swift look at her possessive act, ready as she was then, if she had the strength, to drag him away from the bridal couple— while at the same time she began bubbling away with her congratulations.

'You must be Philip,' said Giles, turning to Croft in

the space Mercy left when she took a second to pause for breath.

And before he could answer, fresh torment arose in her at the reminder that for an age now she hadn't given Philip a thought. She was virtually going under for the second time with the weight of wondering how on earth she was supposed to cling tight to Croft Latimer with Philip around, and almost everyone here knowing she was engaged to Philip. But now Hilary was getting sufficiently over her fear to put in:

'Darling, Mr Arnold, the vicar, has just arrived.'

Yet there was still that beseeching look in her eyes, Mercy noted, even as she made great play of thanking the vicar for a 'simply beautiful service.'

'W-would you like a drink?' Mercy pulled at Croft's arm, taking it on herself to offer him the Drivers' hospitality. It was a relief again to find that he wasn't making any protest as she guided him along the hall and into the largest room where she thought a temporary bar would have been set up.

At the doorway she halted, her eyes doing a feverish tour of the mass of people in there as she looked for Philip. Then she heard from the man she still had by the arm, that there was very little about her that had been missed by him.

'I can wait for a drink,' Croft coolly drawled. 'But from where I'm standing, you certainly look like a young lady sorely in need of one.'

All thoughts of looking for Philip went from her, as straightaway she let go of Croft Latimer's arm. Was it so very obvious what she was up to?

'I—do?' she queried chokily, standing still and looking into those eyes that had looked so very cold, but now appeared to have lost some of their ice.

Her heart picked up a panicky rhythm as Croft Latimer caught hold of her hand and retained it. Oh dear, she thought. It had been natural for her to suppose that to make a play for him was the only way out of this crisis. To make him think he had that certain something that turned her on was a very good way of enabling her, as Hilary had requested, to stick to him like glue. But what she hadn't got round to thinking about was what she did if he took her up on it. But the way his eyes had definitely lost that chill, and the fact that he was still holding on to her hand, had to mean that he was responding, surely?

She was still uncertain whether he was giving assent to the green light she had given him in the possessive way she had caught hold of his arm, when, bending low to speak into her ear above the din, he said:

'You're frozen. I think a nip of brandy wouldn't come amiss.'

He had let go her hand and left her to go over to the bar before she could tell him that she wasn't used to drinking. While she and Philip were saving so hard, they had better things to do with their money than to become regulars at the pub.

She moved a little way into the room, her eyes searching once more as again thoughts of Philip visited her. But she was unable to see him, and before long her mind was once more occupied with her dread of the hours to be got through before she could breathe a thankful sigh and go home.

What she had to concentrate on now, she saw, was that with Croft Latimer thinking she fancied him, and with him not looking averse to the idea—unbelievable as that seemed since she had definitely seen him giving Georgiana the cold shoulder—then did she have it in her to carry on in the long hours to be got though, just as though the two of them could have something in common?

She left her thoughts as a stir in the room caused her to turn, her eyes going to the door. Hilary and Giles had just come in. She saw Hilary's eyes flick over the room as though she was looking for someone. They stopped searching when they lighted on her. But when Hilary didn't come anywhere near, Mercy knew she wanted nothing more from her than to know she was doing as she had been asked.

Because she had to, Mercy smiled a look that said, 'Don't worry—everything is under control'. She saw by the slight nod of her friend's head that her message had been received, even though Hilary did not smile back, her eyes travelling on until they caught sight of Croft Latimer coming away from the crowded bar. It was Mercy's turn to move.

'There's a bit of space over by the French window nobody's grabbed yet,' she said meeting him halfway.

He had one glass only in his hand. He held on to it as he instructed, 'Lead the way.' Then once they were tucked away from the door, he handed her the measure of brandy.

Forgetful that she had had nothing to eat all day, Mercy was of the opinion that if the amber liquid was the cure-all some seemed to think it was, then she had nothing against trying such a remedy for her frayed nerves.

Taking a fair swallow, she looked across the room to where Hilary and Giles were circulating. At the rate they were going it could be an hour before they got round to them, she thought. And if she knew Hilary, she'd soon think of something to ensure that she and Giles by-passed the French window.

'You never said where you live,' she said suddenly off the top of her head, when it appeared Croft wasn't going to be the one to start in with conversation. And then fell to wondering why when flirting seemed to come to other girls so easily, she should find it such uphill work. She forced a smile as teasingly, she asked, 'Is where you live such a great secret?'

'Not at all,' he answered, and favoured her with a

smile of his own, which she discovered held a deal of charm. 'When I'm in this country, I live in London.'

'You travel with your work?' she queried.

'Some,' he replied briefly, which left her searching for what next she should say.

'What sort of work do you do?' she asked, taking another sip of her drink, while thinking this was terrible—only ten minutes of those hours got through and already she was struggling.

'We manufacture communications equipment,' he answered.

And while her mind was starting to boggle—was he anything to do with the Latimer Communications Equipment group? he was advising her to finish her drink, and adding:

'The buffet is under way, can I get you something?'

Mercy refused anything to eat, thinking her stomach just wouldn't be able to cope with anything. 'You go,' she said, meaning not to take her eyes off him in case he made a move in Giles' direction, but wanting some minutes by herself so she could get herself together.

'I think not,' he replied.

She saw his expression was stern, and it caused her to wonder if he intended neither to drink nor eat anything under Hilary's roof. She was still no nearer to knowing what it was he had on Hilary that could terrify her so. But since he had abruptly gone from being a civil if not an easy companion, back to the hard-eyed man she had first seen, she was suddenly eager all at once to do anything that would take that stern look from him, ready to do anything to get his mind off the sole reason he was there.

'Are you anything to do with Latimer Communications Equipment?' she asked, drawing his attention back.

'I run it,' he said, not making a meal of it.

Mercy all but gasped at the revelation he had made

so carelessly. Hilary must have known who he was when she'd told her to stick to him, she thought, incredulous that she, a nonentity who seldom left the village community, should be trying to get him interested in her. Then she had to get over her incredulity, for he was going on to say:

'That's me dealt with. How about you, Mercy Yeomans? Do you live around here? What sort of work do *you* do?'

Steadily the minutes ticked by as Mercy battled to keep her end up. Not that Croft Latimer belittled anything of what she had to tell him. But knowing who he was, the type of female he must be used to spending his time with, even though he hadn't taken Georgiana up on her overtures, she was conscious that there must be only a thin line between her managing to keep him entertained, and his experiencing utter boredom.

Yet he didn't appear to be bored. Miraculously he hadn't given her a look such as she had seen him give Georgiana, but had listened attentively when she had given him chapter and verse about her job. And had shown interest, too, when she had told him of her parents, now living in Australia.

The slow-ticking minutes had turned into an hour, time appearing to pick up speed once the cake had been cut, champagne handed round, and speeches made. But the whole time there was fear, communicated to her from Hilary, that sometime soon Croft would suddenly leave her side, or if not leave, speak up from where he stood, and that all her efforts would be in vain.

But as more time passed, Mercy began to be hopeful that now the dangerous moment was gone, that moment when the speeches were done, that Croft had forgotten about his purpose in being there that day. Though she knew that she dared not cease her vigil yet—there was still time.

'Hello, Mercy.'

She turned her head, smothering a sigh as she saw Hilary's brother had come over to them. 'Hello, Justin,' she said politely, only too well aware that it was better to be friendly to him than risk his playing some trick by way of getting his own back for some thoughtless remark. He had that sort of mentality, she considered—or maybe it was a phase all sixteen-year-olds went through.

'The catering staff are run off their feet,' he said, smiling pleasantly and handing her a tall glass of clear liquid. 'I've brought you a drink.'

'Why, thank you, Justin,' she replied, and took a wary sip to find it was nothing more innocuous than lemonade.

'Can I get something for you, sir?' Justin asked Croft with equal pleasantness.

Croft declined, but as Justin made no move to go, regardless that Croft had stated he didn't want to be introduced to anyone, Mercy felt duty bound to perform this function. And when Justin remained pleasant, respectful, as the two shook hands, she could only think then that either he had been well threatened by his father that morning, or that he had straight away seen that Croft was more than a match for him if he tried any of his sauce with him.

As soon as she had finished her thirst-quenching lemonade, however, Justin, still being angelically polite, took her glass and excused himself.

But no sooner had he gone than he was back. 'Phone call for you, Mercy,' he said, and as she had suspected it might, his front started to slip though he still managed to look innocent. 'Shall I tell him you're otherwise—engaged?'

For seconds that tongue-in-cheek look of Justin's that she knew so well, had her puzzled, causing her to wonder if it was her overwrought nerves that were making her unusually slow off the mark. Then as 'Tell *him*! Engaged!' sorted itself out in her bewildered brain, she was suddenly appalled—how could she have forgotten all about Philip!

Aghast that it must be hours since she had given Philip a thought, Mercy automatically told Justin she would take the call. But she was then torn in two with trying to remember the last time she had seen Hilary; or, more importantly, Giles.

'You can take the call in the library,' Justin hinted when she made no move to go, but stood dithering as she wondered if it was safe to leave Croft Latimer for a few minutes. 'It's quiet in there,' he added, a look on his face that was wiser than his years.

Without knowing it, for Croft could not be aware of her indecision, she thought, it was he himself who settled her dilemma.

'I'll come with you if I may,' he said easily, having put a stop to her dithering only to make her feel edgy that he might, in the quiet of the library, be going to take heed of Justin's second hint. That was before, a sardonic curve to his mouth, he said, 'There's a phone call I should like to make myself.'

Relief mingled with a feeling of embarrassment as with Croft close behind her she crossed the room, all too well aware that the eyes of many people known to her were on her. She hoped with all her heart Philip would understand when she told him why it was she had clung like a leech to the side of Croft Latimer. And only hoped she could get to him first. It would be all over the village tomorrow, she didn't doubt that—it didn't bear thinking about.

It was some time since she had been in the Drivers' library, but even so, she would have thought she should have remembered which door to go through. No wonder her brain had dulled, she thought, as she stood in the hall with Croft, trying to make up her mind where the library lay. Although he was a witty and an

easy conversationalist, she had had to remember the
part she was playing—and unused as she was to flirting,
that hadn't come easily.

'This door, I should think,' he said, again coming to
the rescue, as he indicated the only door that was
closed.

Mercy saw the phone was off the hook as soon as she
entered the room. And only then did she have any
feeling of urgency as she hurried over to the telephone
table, Croft's voice coming to her as she picked up the
phone, 'If you want to be private I can . . .'

'Oh no,' she said, her anxiety for Giles back with her.
'It won't be anything important.'

She watched him go to close the door, then she was
giving what concentration she could muster to Philip at
the other end of the phone; who, for once, was sounding
resentful that he'd had to wait so long.

'I thought it might have crossed your mind to give
me a ring when you noticed I wasn't there,' he said, the
moment he had received her apology for keeping him
waiting.

'I did think of it,' she heard herself lying, feeling
slightly scandalised as she did so, for she had never had
occasion to lie to Philip. 'B-but I didn't want to disturb
your mother if she was—er—resting,' she further
invented. And she saw again then what a love Philip
was, that not only had he believed her, but that he had
forgiven her too.

'I left ringing you until now because I didn't want
anyone to fetch you away while all the telegrams were
being read out,' he said, showing what a thoughtful
person he was. 'I hated to let you down, Mercy, but I
knew you would understand. It's Mother.'

He then went on to tell her how, as Mrs Bailey had
been getting out of his car last night, she had turned her
foot and suffered a very severe sprain.

'I just couldn't leave her,' he apologised. 'Naturally

Mother said I should, she said she would be all right, but with every movement painful to her,' he broke off to tell her of Mrs Bailey dropping her knitting when he was about to leave for the church, and how the pain had been too terrible for her to move to pick it up, and how that had decided things for him.

'You couldn't do anything else,' Mercy consoled, feeling something of a hypocrite because, as things had turned out, it was just as well he wasn't there.

'I knew you'd understand,' he said. Then went on, 'But I've managed to contact Mrs Vialls, and she has promised to come over early tomorrow and stay with Mother until we get back, so it won't spoil our arrangements for the morning.'

From the corner of her eye Mercy saw Croft had finished his inspection of the bookshelves and had now turned his attention on her. And what she and Philip had planned for the following morning was forgotten as it occurred to her that if she was to keep Croft's attention, the best way to do it was not to be heard dallying on the phone with some other man.

'I'll . . .' look forward to it, she had been going to say. 'I'll have to go now,' she said instead. 'Someone else is waiting to use the phone.' And Philip, kind, considerate soul that he was, did not need a bigger hint than that.

'I'll see you tomorrow then. Enjoy the wedding,' he said. 'Bye for now.'

'Bye, Philip,' she said. Then she had to struggle to remember her role, for Croft Latimer, one eyebrow arching skywards, was asking:

'Philip? Do I have competition?'

'Grief—no,' she heard herself say, and had to wonder that she could sound so dismissive of the man she was going to marry next year.

Shame hit her at that point. Confusion too. She had been doing her darnedest to get Croft Latimer sufficiently interested to forget all about the scene he had come there to make, and now the fact he was querying the 'competition' made it fairly obvious his thoughts were going along the channels she had wanted.

'I'll leave you to make your call in . . .' she began, already on her way. Then felt his hand on her arm, moving down to take hold of her hand.

'My call won't take a minute,' he said, his eyes steady on hers. 'But first . . .'

It was at that point that she knew he was going to kiss her. At that point she came near to breaking down.

'It-it's a bit early in the day for th-that sort of thing,' she stammered, backing away as far as his hold on her hand would allow. She saw the way his face had resumed its stern lines, as after a swift glance at his watch, he said:

'Disregard the fact it's going on for eight. Disregard the fact that there is no set time for one's natural instincts to have an outlet. Tell me straight, Mercy Yeomans, have I spent the last few hours with an old-fashioned girl—or are you by way of being a grade one tease?'

Fresh confusion hit her, and she was thankful that some time had elapsed since she had drunk that brandy and toasted the bride in champagne. She needed a clear head to assemble what it was she thought Croft was saying. She could not avoid the thought that he had bed in mind. Surely that was what he was asking? But she knew herself at a loss as to how to answer him. If she agreed to the former, said she was old-fashioned, then she *would* have blown it—he would drop her like a hot brick, she didn't need to be told that. He would probably go straight from this room and, disgruntled to have wasted so much time with her, would assuredly create that scene Hilary was so petrified of.

'Is—er—anybody—old-fashioned, these days?' she answered, thoughts of Hilary, of having her ruined marriage on her conscience, fixed in her mind.

'You're admitting you're a tease?'

'I'm—saying—I don't like to be rushed,' she answered, drowning in a conversation she had never dreamed she would ever be a party to.

And relief rose again when she saw that aggressive look leave him. 'I take your point,' he said, his mouth beginning to curve. 'You're saying it's early yet, but who knows what might happen later?'

Feeling easier that for the moment she had been let off the hook, not that he would have done more than kiss her, when they could well have been interrupted, she thought, her answer to Croft was a speaking smile. Let him read what he would into that. As soon as the party broke up, she would be speeding off to her flat— Croft Latimer would never know in which direction her car had gone.

Croft smiled too, a definite gleam in his eye, she thought, as still keeping her with him, he laid the phone on the table and with one hand still holding her hand, he dialled, then put the receiver to his ear.

She had no idea who he was calling, and cared even less. Though the brevity of his, 'He's all yours if you want him,' the, 'Yes—she did,' before he put down the phone, made her wonder if his call had been strictly necessary. Though no doubt the person at the other end had been able to make something of his telephone shorthand.

Leaving the library, by unspoken mutual consent, they investigated one of the other rooms where music mingled with shrieks and laughter. It was here that Mercy saw the younger element from among the guests, plus a sprinkling of young-at-heart aunts and uncles, arms and legs going out at all angles as most of them caught the beat of the music.

'Dance?' queried Croft, turning to her.

Rapidly running out of small talk, far from comfortable with the tack their conversation had taken in the library, Mercy thought it was the best suggestion she had heard in a long while.

Lack of practice had caused her to think she was not a very good dancer, so she was surprised to find she was actually enjoying dancing with Croft. And when they came away from the cleared area when the tape finished, there was a faint flush on her cheeks from her exertions.

'I enjoyed that!' she exclaimed, glad to be able to be honest about something with the man.

It seemed as though Croft had enjoyed it too, from the way his eyes were warm as they searched her face with its obvious sincerity. But if he had been going to make any reply, before he could do so, Justin had come up to them, another tall glass, of orange squash this time, in his hand, which he handed to her with the words:

'I thought you were looking a shade hot, Mercy.'

Thirsty, and realising when he waited for her glass that they must have had a run on glasses and were short of them, she made short work of the orange. And over the next two hours, whenever she looked in the least bit pink-cheeked, Justin would attentively appear with a drink for her. Mercy began to change her opinion of the boy—he couldn't, she thought, be such a bad lad after all.

By the time ten o'clock came round, she realised she was having a great time. For one thing Croft had refrained from making any leading remark, so that she was well on the way to forgetting he had in fact said anything that she should be wary about.

They had just come off the floor, Justin again there with a brimming glass. She took it from him, but this time contented herself with only a sip. She was feeling light-headed, she suddenly realised, and was having to concentrate really hard on why that should be. Of course, she had eaten nothing that day, she recalled. It wasn't any wonder with all the dancing she had been doing. She must fast be using up her energy reserves.

'Would you like to sit down?'

The suggestion came from Croft. It caused her to wonder if her disappearing energy had been noted by him.

'No, I don't think so,' she said, her brow wrinkling as the thought came that she had something to do, but couldn't quite remember what it was. 'I—have to go somewhere.'

She emptied the glass in her hand, and left him to go out into the hall, knowing he would think she was going to the powder room. But she wasn't going to the powder room. Her brain felt like so much cotton wool, but she knew she had to see Hilary about something.

Suddenly her head started to spin, causing her to grab at the wall for support. Something to eat, she thought, trying to remember in which direction the buffet lay.

'Where's Croft Latimer?'

The sharply spoken words had her leaving the wall, her eyes making out what looked like two Hilarys standing in front of her.

'I was—looking for you,' she said.

'Where is he?' was hissed back at her.

'Giles . . .'

'No, idiot—Croft Latimer. Pull yourself together, for heaven's sake.'

She didn't know why Hilary should call her an idiot, why she should be telling her to pull herself together—it offended her. She moved from the wall, her body erect.

'He's in the other room,' she said stiffly. 'The dancing room.'

'Then for goodness' sake take him away,' said Hilary. 'Really, Mercy, it's years since I've asked a favour of you, surely you can do this for me.'

Mercy melted. Poor Hilary was sounding quite hysterical.

'Take him away?' she repeated.

'Get him out of here.'

'Wh-where shall I take him?'

'What the hell do I care where you take him? People are beginning to trickle away now. You won't be missed. Just get him out of here so I can know some peace.'

'But—how do I do that?'

Though her thoughts seemed to be taking a long time to get themselves together, Mercy had a clear picture of Croft Latimer, stern and immovable. If he didn't want to go, she was very clear about one thing, there was nothing she could do to make him.

'Oh, for God's sake! Where have you been this last five years—in a nunnery?'

Mercy was ready to take offence again. Then from somewhere came the reminder that Hilary was her best friend, her best friend and that she was in trouble.

'Leave it to me,' she said stoutly, and turned, grabbed the wall again until the world righted itself, and was then ready to go the way she had come.

Justin was hovering, looking for her, when she went back into the room. And realising suddenly that her throat felt parched, she started to hope he hadn't found anyone else to give that lemonade to before he spotted her.

'Are you all right?'

She looked up to see Croft was there at her elbow. 'I'm fine,' she answered. Then seeing the reason for his enquiry as Justin at that moment saw her and started to make his way across, she thought she had better explain. 'Ac-actually,' she said, her tongue feeling as though it didn't belong to her, 'I haven't eaten today. I think—my blood sugar level must be—at zero.'

'In that case,' he said, stretching out his hand and taking the lemonade Justin was about to hand her, 'I think we'd better save this until you've had something solid inside you.'

It irritated her as Justin floated away, that Croft Latimer was tryng to deprive her of the lemonade her throat felt parched for. Without fuss, she took it away from him and took a swallow. She felt better then, and let him take the glass from her. All the time there was something spinning round in her head about a favour she had to do for Hilary.

The floor moved, or she thought it did. She grabbed hold of Croft to steady herself, then quite clearly remembered Hilary didn't want him at her wedding.

'Ac-actually,' she said, still holding on to him in case the floor moved again, 'I was thinking of going home. Would you like to come with me?'

She felt his hand on her elbow, and knew he had accepted her invitation as she walked across the cushion of the floor. He had the front door open and she could hear the rain pelting down, even if she couldn't see it. Her mind went on to the bacon and eggs she would cook when she got home. It was only fair, she thought, that she cooked some for him too. He hadn't eaten anything either, as far as she could remember. He must be starving too.

'Wait here,' Croft instructed when she was almost smelling the frying bacon. 'I'll bring the car round.'

She caught his sleeve just as he was about to leave her, her mind on the question of whether he would like one egg or two.

'You won't have to—go home straight away—when we get to my flat, will you?' she said. And meaning to tell him about the supper she had planned, 'We can share something—l-lovely there—if you can st-stay.'

She thought he said, 'The state you're in I've had better offers,' but he had disengaged his arm and gone before she could ask him to repeat it.

And she was still trying to make sense of what she thought he had said—what state? what offer? when he was back taking her arm and putting her into his car.

CHAPTER THREE

IT was with a thundering head that Mercy opened her eyes the following morning. She winced as a shaft of sunlight pierced them, and closed her eyes again.

I'll get up and take some aspirin in a minute, she thought. But unable to so much as remember getting into bed last night, she was unable to remember ever having woken up to feel so wretched. Even to go in search of aspirin for her throbbing head seemed too much of an effort.

With her eyes closed to keep out the light, she tugged at what memory she did have. Croft Latimer had brought her home, she managed to recall. Recalled, too, that the motion of his car had made her feel quite ill. Which was odd in itself because she had never been car sick before, and if her stirring memory was working accurately, he had the sort of car that purred along, rather than rattling like her own.

She concentrated on what had happened after that. After he had stopped his car outside her flat. But there was little to remember. He had asked her for her key, she dragged up hazily from somewhere. Though he hadn't understood her when she had tried to tell him it was beneath the plant pot; he couldn't have done, because he had taken matters into his own hands and had taken hold of her bag and found her key amongst all the paraphernalia it housed. He must then, she thought, have opened up her flat, pushed her inside, and gone back to London.

The question then came: how did she come to have her handbag, since the last time she had seen it had been when she had left it in Hilary's bedroom before

48

going to the church? And the answer was that someone could have handed it to her when she left, she supposed. But she shelved the problem as, her headache growing out of all proportion, she decided she would just have to get out of bed and get those pain-killers.

But it was precisely at that moment that a movement in the bed beside her shocked her into rigid awareness that she had company. And so cataclysmic was her shock, that for several seconds, she forgot completely about her headache.

Sitting up abruptly, she turned her eyes to that companion. And as what colour she did have drained away, she saw that the man she thought had pushed her inside her flat last night and gone on his way—had not gone on his way.

'*You*!' she croaked, and winced with pain as her temples renewed their pounding. Then, 'Oh—*no*!' as the most shattering of all revelations struck as he joined her in a sitting position.

For his chest was naked, and as her eyes went hurriedly from him, she saw that the rest of him must be naked too if the pile of masculine garments festooning her bedroom chair was anything to go by.

'Oh no,' she said again, her voice a whisper, as amused grey eyes took in her incredulous expression.

'Yes, me,' mocked Croft Latimer. 'Can you not remember saying goodnight?'

'I c-can't remember—a thing,' she stammered hoarsely, not wanting to believe what was so blatantly obvious.

'Which isn't surprising, considering the condition you were in,' he said easily, looking quite relaxed, where shock still kept her rigid.

'Condition!' she echoed, not ready to believe any of this was happening—to *her*! Not believing her eyes that he was so unconcerned, careless of the magnitude of what had happened, that he could adjust his position and casually lean back against the headboard.

'To put it mildly, you were carrying a full load,' he told her.

'Carrying . . .? You mean—I was drunk!'

Shock started to depart as anger licked into life at his cool assertion. And before he could confirm that was indeed what he had meant, she was saying heatedly, regardless that it wasn't doing her throbbing head any good:

'Don't be ridiculous! All I drank at the wedding apart from that brandy and a glass of champagne, was watered down fruit juice.'

'Plus the double vodka I saw Justin upend into your drink on at least one occasion. That on an empty stomach . . .'

'Vodka!'

His look was speculative. 'You sound surprised. Didn't you have a prior arrangement with that young man? I thought . . .'

'I know what you thought,' The mammoth shock she had received was sending her out of control. Though if what Croft had said was true, some of her anger had to be for Hilary's brother. 'I'll kill that Justin,' she raged, still aghast at what, through him and his juvenile tricks, so very dreadfully had happened.

'You're saying you didn't put him up to lacing your drinks?'

'Of course I didn't,' she snapped, and her anger vented only on him as the enormity of what *had* happened grew in her, 'And you're no better.'

Perhaps nothing had happened, nudged a small voice. But seeing Croft lying there, cool, relaxed, unanswering, his broad shoulders no myth now she had full view of them without so much as a shirt on, the hair on his chest a shade darker than his fair head, she wondered what chance there was of that. The thought tempered her anger, even if the virile look of him was telling her—no chance.

'You ...' She hesitated, unable for a moment to bring it out. Afraid of his confirmation—yet needing desperately to know. 'You ...' she hesitated again. Then was angry with herself as well as him, and was then storming in to challenge:

'You took advantage of me.'

'I did?'

Hope rose. 'Didn't you?'

He didn't answer straight away, and his face gave nothing away as he looked coolly back at her. He must know what I'm asking, she thought, and wasn't sure she wouldn't physically set about him if he didn't soon tell her.

Hope died the moment she saw a crooked grin appear on his features. 'With you throwing yourself at me the way you did?' he shrugged. 'I'm only a mere male, after all.'

She went pink, her worst suspicions confirmed. And he was right, she had rather thrown herself at him. But that didn't stop her from feeling sick inside.

And then anger had hold of her once more, and was there to clamp down her sickness. He *had* taken advantage of her. He must have known she wasn't in any condition to resist. Yet still he had ...

She hated him then. Hated him more than she had hated anybody. And if she had been—loving—to him last night, then she was ready to show him this morning, that far from turning her on, loathsome expression, he would very soon learn that he wasn't her type at all.

'Get out of my bed,' she ordered for a start. And then coloured furiously as knowledge returned that he must be naked under the covers. 'No! Stay where you are,' she countermanded, her eyes going frantically in search of her robe.

A quick glance down the front of her showed she still had on her full length petticoat, but unused to flitting round in gentlemen's company in flimsy undergarments, she didn't have the nerve for the moment to get out of bed and search for her errant robe.

'Anything to oblige a lady,' came Croft's mocking reply, as he stayed where he was.

'You might as well know now,' she threw out, seeing no reason why she should spare his feelings after what he had so criminally done, 'that—that all over you I might have seemed, but that in actual fact I never—not for a single moment—fancied you.'

'What a most peculiar way you have of showing it,' was the cool sardonic answer she could have done without.

'As a matter of fact,' she said, colouring again but determined to ignore any of his innuendoes, 'had it not been for Hilary begging me to stick to you like glue, I would never have approached you the way I did. You, Mr Latimer,' she ended with a flourish, 'just don't appeal to me—that way.'

There, she thought, chew on that. Hilary and Giles must be on their way to the airport by now, there wasn't a thing Croft Latimer could do to ruin the start of their marriage.

But he was not at all put out by what she had said, she saw. And it was she, not he, who was astounded when, his sardonic manner gone, he had a revelation of his own to make, as he stunned her with:

'And do you suppose, Miss Yeomans, that I wasn't aware of that the whole time?'

'You—knew!' He was lying. He had to be. He was only saying that to save his face. . . .

'Do you suppose I didn't see your friend was running scared from the moment she stated her last-minute desire to have each of her bridesmaids photographed with her separately in turn?' And not a grin, a smile, about him. 'I knew then that one of you would be delegated to keep tabs on me—the surprise was, that it turned out to be you.'

Mercy grasped that he had bounced back her comment that she hadn't fancied him. He wasn't disguising that he thought she, with her unsophisticated way, her minimum of make-up, her countrified air, was the last person a man like him would take a fancy to. She was forced to believe what he had just told her, that he had been wise to her from the start. Just as she believed he had more than got his own back on her for the way she had tried to pull the wool over his eyes. Oh why, why, *why* hadn't Hilary asked Pamela or Georgiana to keep tabs on him?

There seemed nothing more to be said. She wanted him to go. But first the embarrassment of getting out of this bed had to be overcome. About to turn on her side where she couldn't see him, about to tell him to clear out, she suddenly became rigid with panic again at a sound from the other side of the door. And suddenly she was clutching on to his arm that lay on top of the covers without knowing she had, for she heard a voice she instantly recognised as Philip's as it came through the wood panelling.

'Mercy!' he called.

And then, while she sat there as though hypnotised staring at the door handle, there came a tap on the door, and quietly, with the consideration that was second nature to Philip in case she was still asleep, slowly the door handle turned.

Philip was in the room, had started to say, 'Your door-bell's gone again . . .' before red colour flushed his cheeks and he stared uncomprehendingly at a white-faced Mercy who had lost the power of speech, and at the fit, bare-chested, all male specimen, who looked right back at him without so much as a blink.

'*Mercy!*' Philip's shocked tones went through her as she became mesmerised by his Adam's apple working overtime. 'How *could* you! How *could* you!'

Stunned, incapable of answering, unable to excuse what she had done, Mercy couldn't bear to see the terrible shock in her fiancé's face. Her ashen cheeks flamed into shamed colour, and she turned her gaze to Croft, as though hoping he would help her out.

But if she was too ashamed to look at Philip, there was not an atom of shame in the man who just lay there as if to imply that the ceiling would have to fall in before he would have anything to say. Croft Latimer, she saw, was as cool and as relaxed as ever as his eyes stayed on Philip, not looking as if he was in any way discomfited to be caught so. He looked, she thought, more as if he was dissecting the other man, and deciding he was in no way worth troubling himself over.

Her eyes swung back to Philip and her heart went out to him as she saw him swallow again, and heard his cry of, 'Oh, Mercy. You were saving yourself for me.' And again, 'How *could* you,' before, as quietly as he had come in, he went out.

Vaguely the memory came that she and Philip had planned to go to the early session at the swimming baths in Channing that morning. But she was still too stunned to move when he had gone, and she sat staring in horror at the door he had closed behind him. It was only when she felt a stomach reaction, no time for embarrassment at the flimsiness of her attire, that she moved.

To be ignominiously sick on top of everything else, just about put the tin lid on it, she thought, uncaring then what she looked like as Croft Latimer, having donned his trousers, followed her rocket trail into the bathroom.

'Sit there for a minute,' he advised, taking hold of her arm when her performance was over, and pushing her to sit on the edge of the bath.

Like a child, she dumbly suffered his administering a warm damp face cloth to her face, and had no word for him either as he pushed back her hair from her brow. She stared solemnly back at him when grey eyes wandered over her every feature, from her smooth pale forehead, to her petite nose and generous mouth, and then back to her stunned eyes again.

He left her, but only briefly. And returned bearing the dressing gown she hadn't been able to see earlier. 'Put this round you,' he instructed, but was already helping her into it. She felt his hand touch her bare shoulder, and instinct made her knock it away.

'How are you feeling now?' he enquired, unperturbed, his voice not unkind.

'Great, just great,' she replied with a tone of sarcasm.

'So I hear.' He didn't sound as though her sarcasm bothered him any, for his voice was light and easy when he suggested pleasantly, 'Come into the other room, I'll make you a cup of tea.'

Wanting to tell him to stay out of her kitchen, he'd done more than enough for her thank you very much, Mercy simply didn't feel she had the energy. She submitted to being led into her sitting room and settled into one of her two easy chairs, Croft then disappearing into her kitchen. She let him get on with it. Her head was throbbing so badly she would have loved to go back to bed, or alternatively to be able to lie down somewhere.

It was odd what thoughts came to you in moments of crisis, she thought, her mind leaving the situation which by her own efforts she had got herself into, to ponder on the settee that had made up the three-piece suite from her parents' home, but which she'd had to make the choice and part with because there had simply not been enough room in her flat for the large three-seater and the two chairs. If she had that settee now, she rather thought she would be making full use of it.

Though would she? Dreadful though she felt, she couldn't see herself stretching out anywhere until Croft Latimer had taken himself off.

'If I know anything about being hungover, you'll be needing these.'

She looked up to see he was now wearing his shirt, and that it was not the cup of tea she had been promised he was handing her, but a glass containing a couple of dissolving aspirins.

'You've been raking about in my bathroom cabinet,' she said, but without heat, as she took the glass from him.

'In the circumstances I didn't think you'd mind.'

She had swallowed the medication when Croft next came back, and was part way to feeling isolated from any of what had gone on as she watched him draw up a small table, place two cups of tea upon it, and then take the easy chair opposite her, before he commented:

'From the look of you I'd say you could do with a whole heap of sugar, but I guessed you prefer your tea without.'

'Genius,' she muttered.

'Going to take it out on me that the boy-friend has a key to your flat and knows his way to your bedroom?'

His voice had been mild, but there had been a note there that put her back up, even if it was defensively, and she told him:

'Of course he knows where my bedroom is. It was Philip who helped me with the furniture when I moved in. And he doesn't have a key to this flat . . .' Her voice tailed off, 'I keep a key under the plant pot outside'

'So that was what you were babbling on about last night,' he said. 'That was Philip, was it?' And a mocking note there she didn't want to hear, 'I see what you meant when you said I didn't have any competition.'

'How dare . . .' she started to fly out, a picture of Philip's stricken face haunting her. She broke off, wincing, her head just not ready yet to accompany her into battle. 'For your information,' she told him coldly, 'Philip and I are . . .' her voice faltered as she corrected, 'were, engaged.'

Without looking at her left hand, Croft was quick to observe bluntly, 'You don't wear an engagement ring.'

'A person can be engaged without wearing a ring,' she snapped. And on the defensive again, and hating that he could do this to her, 'We were saving. Philip thought ... We both thought,' she found herself correcting again, 'that an engagement ring was an unnecessary expense.'

What his opinion on that was, she never learned. 'How long have you and this—thrifty swain—been engaged?' he asked instead. It was nothing to do with him, in her opinion, yet she found herself answering before she could think.

'Nearly a year.' Then, realisation there again, she looked at him mutinously. 'But I'm no longer engaged. Thanks to you, I doubt if Philip will ever speak to me again.'

Far from looking abashed, or in the very least contrite, she saw that Croft Latimer was looking as though he thought he had done her something of a favour. So she was not any nearer to feeling in an agreeable frame of mind when, with a careless shrug, he remarked:

'You'll soon make it up.'

'Not after what he saw in there,' she retorted, indicating the bedroom.

'Oh, come now, Mercy, surely you're allowed one little lapse.'

One little lapse! Was that all he saw it as? An engaged girl being found in bed with another man! By her fiancé!

She threw him a withering look. And had a distinct impression as he looked back, the epitome of innocence, that he didn't really believe what he was saying. From nowhere it came to her that he would expect any woman he got himself engaged to, to treat that engagement as sacrosanct. It underlined for her, since it wasn't his engagement that had been broken, that he was treating what had happened much too lightly.

'Far from being "one little lapse"', she told him with some heat, 'it was my only lapse. And,' she said, determined to make him see it wasn't some trivial matter as far as she was concerned, 'a lapse Philip will consider unforgivable.'

About to add, primly, that she herself considered it unforgivable too, she saw the corner of Croft's mouth twitch, and the words dried up. She knew before he spoke that she was not going to like what he said.

'Paragon of virtue, is he—this Philip?' And before she could get in to defend him, 'You're saying that since you've been engaged he has never been tempted to bed another woman.'

'No, he has not,' she said stoutly, and, stung by the thought that it looked as if he was suggesting she wasn't woman enough to keep Philip from straying, 'He's never been to bed with any woman.'

She stopped, aghast. How could she be talking of Philip in this way? Revealing such private things about the man she had up until an hour ago thought she would be marrying next year! She looked across at Croft, intending to throw him a look of searing dislike. But the expression on his face, nothing short of incredulity, made her re-charge her batteries to overspill acid on to him if he made just one crack about Philip and his virgin state.

'Truly a paragon,' he muttered, though more to himself than to her, she thought. And before she could fire, he was saying, still incredulous, 'You've been engaged for nearly a year and the only time he dallied in your bedroom was to carry furniture!'

'You have proof of that, haven't you?' she answered sourly, looking away from him, not for the first time wondering how the girl she thought herself to be, should now be having a conversation that was so alien to her. And then, suddenly, hope was there again. Surely, with Croft questioning if she and Philip had—had anticipated their marriage, then—surely it must mean . . .

She looked at him, saw he was looking thoughtful. Then hope was dashed again, when his face creased into the most infuriating grin, and he said cheerfully:

'You mean the proof I have that I was—er—first with you?' And while her heart sank, he even had the audacity to emit a short laugh, before, just as cheerfully, he insolently questioned, 'What's wrong with the chap—afraid you'll lose all respect for him if he lets you have your way with him, is he?'

Mercy was out of her chair, disregarding her thumping head. 'That's not funny,' she blazed. And fairly spluttering with rage that he thought Philip highly comical, 'Not all men are like you. He would never have taken advantage of a girl who didn't know what she was doing.'

She was still boiling when with a casual ease Croft got to his feet, his bantering look vanishing, his eyes narrowing as she told him:

'I've had just about enough of you, Croft Latimer. Go back to wherever you came from. We don't need your sort round here. We may be a sleepy community, but at least we do know something about common forms of decency . . .'

'Smug piety, I would have said,' he interrupted her brusquely. 'And if you're suggesting I should not have stayed with you last night, just remember I would never have done so without your very forthcoming invitation.'

'I . . .'

It was as far as she could go. She had no memory of inviting him to stay, but could easily have done so, she thought. But she refused this time to give way to shame. He was an experienced man of the world. He must have known she was in no condition to know what she had been doing.

'Well, you ...' she started to fire up, only to be chopped off as he added silkily, his own ill-humour gone:

'And surely, you aren't going to call me a cad, when *you*, my dear, were the one who forgot to tell me you were engaged?'

Floored, Mercy threw him a seething look. 'I'm going to get dressed,' she said stiffly. 'I hope to find you gone when I get back.'

In the bathroom, she fumed against men like Croft Latimer. But no matter how she fumed, by the time she had washed and donned trousers and a blouse, she knew that no amount of fuming would undo all that had been done.

She caught sight of her pale face in the bathroom mirror; no hint of colour there in a clear complexion that had been commented on as being beautiful. Her pallor didn't surprise her—if it was a hangover she had, then she'd make doubly sure she never had another one. She looked at her face in the mirror again, not seeing her perfect bone structure, the slightly hollow cheeks many a model would have coveted.

Apart from her pallor, she didn't look any different from the way she had looked yesterday, she saw. She sighed, realised her headache was beginning to fade, then wondered how she had expected to look. She couldn't remember a thing about the night she had shared with Croft Latimer, so how could she expect to see the light of experience in her eyes?

Her mind drifted on until she caught herself wondering; had she undressed herself, or had he done it for her? And then there was instant hot colour flushing her cheeks. Hastily she backed from the mirror, unable to face herself, unable to let her mind wonder further.

The smell of bacon frying hit her the moment she

came from the bathroom. And she didn't know which annoyed her more, the fact that he was still in the flat, or that he had calmly commandeered her kitchen. In no way friendly, she went to sort him out.

'I hope you don't mind,' he threw over his shoulder before she could get started. 'I never go anywhere without breakfast.'

'Sorry I'm not like your usual lady-friends,' she snapped waspishly. 'They always cook breakfast for you, I suppose.'

He sent her a smile of some warmth, charm only about him. 'Invariably,' he agreed. 'Do you prefer your bacon crisp or raw at the edges?'

Staggered by his cool cheek, Mercy found herself replying, 'Crisp,' which wasn't what she had been going to say at all. And all at once through the fog of oblivion came a trace of remembrance. 'Bacon and egg,' she said, the way in which she said it causing Croft to divert his attention from the frying pan to her.

'Bacon and egg?' he prompted.

'I've just remembered,' she said, sinking down on to the nearest kitchen chair. 'When I invited you back here, it was because I was hungry, I thought you would be hungry too. I was going to cook bacon and egg for us both!'

For several long seconds Croft studied her downcast face. But his attention had returned to the frying pan, when quietly he answered, 'So that was the something "lovely" you invited me to stay for?'

Glumly Mercy didn't reply. What was the point in going through all that again? What was done was done. That it had resulted in her being minus a fiancé, was something she would have to come to terms with later.

'Eat that up,' Croft instructed, placing a plate of crisply done bacon and a perfectly cooked egg in front of her. He then put his own plate down on the table and took the chair facing her.

Mechanically she picked up the knife and fork he had provided. The bacon smelled delicious, and she realised she was ravenous. Slowly she began to eat, her thoughts too depressed for conversation.

'Buck up,' Croft said, sounding much too cheerful to her in her present frame of mind.

It was all right for him! As soon as he'd eaten the breakfast he never went anywhere without, he would be on his way. He didn't have to stay and face the news of *his* broken engagement being everyone's property.

'It can't be as bad as all that,' he cut into her thoughts.

'Can't it?' she said sourly, flicking him an unsmiling look and away again. 'You don't know Ravensmere.'

'You mean tongues will wag.'

'They'll have a field day.'

'You're positive you won't become reconciled with your fiancé?'

'Ex-fiancé,' she threw across the table shortly, and left it at that.

'He's the sort who will blab it all over the village?' Croft probed.

'Oh no,' she said, jerked out of her despondency. 'Philip Bailey's too good, too kind, ever to be spiteful. Though,' she hesitated, 'though he'll have to tell his mother something, and—and he's never lied to his mother.'

'Saint, is he?'

She ignored him, her mind flinching from what Mrs Bailey would make of it all. Philip's mother had never liked her, she knew that. And sprained foot or no sprained foot, it wouldn't stop her from putting the boot in over the phone.

'Mrs Vialls . . .' she said, speaking her thoughts out loud as she remembered that Philip had only been able to call that morning because Mrs Vialls, the village newspaper, had been going to sit with his mother.

'Mrs Vialls?'

'The local intelligence service.'

Briefly Mercy explained why Philip hadn't been at the wedding yesterday, telling Croft of Mrs Bailey's sprained foot, and how Mrs Vialls had been going to stay with her that morning to allow Philip some free time.

'She must have got round there at the crack of dawn to enable Bailey to call here so early,' he commented.

'The press never sleep,' she said, with wry humour, and saw she had amused him. She decided it wasn't funny. 'Philip and I were going to go to the early session at the swimming baths in the next town,' she said flatly.

'That something else you've just remembered?'

'I didn't set my alarm for it, did I?' she retorted.

'Neither you did,' he said pleasantly, and returned to the subject of Mrs Vialls. 'It worries you what this old trout spreads around the village? That you'll have to hang your head in shame?'

Mercy gave him a speaking look. He had gone from being serious to treating the whole thing as something to poke fun at. 'Of course it does,' she said, disgruntled. He had never lived in a village, that was clear. She would never live it down. Why, in twenty years' time she would still be pointed out as the girl who had latched on to one of the guests at Hilary Driver's wedding, the girl who had taken him home with her and let him stay all night.

Dejectedly she pushed her plate away. She recalled the sly look or two she had received at the wedding yesterday, and saw then that once everyone knew her engagement was at an end, they would soon make up what they didn't know and treat it as gospel.

'You know, Mercy Yeomans,' said Croft, suddenly interrupting her mental torture, 'to my mind you seem far more upset at what people will say, than you are that your love has flown.'

'Darn you,' she flared. 'How could you know how I feel? You'll be flying too, won't you?' She bit down on 'the sooner the better', she thought she had made that fairly obvious. 'You won't have to face any of the people who up until yesterday were expecting wedding bells to ring for me next.'

'Good grief!' he exclaimed, reading something in her flash of anger that had never been there. 'You're not by any unthinkable chance suggesting I do the "decent thing' and marry you myself, are you?' And while she looked at him, her astonishment matching his own, he added, his expression grim, 'You couldn't think of anything as diabolical as that—could you?'

'Marry *you*!' All the contempt she was capable of was in those two words. When she married she wanted a considerate, thoughtful man, not someone like this hard cynic. 'Don't bother to wash up,' she added disdainfully, not wrapping up her hint that she didn't want him to delay his departure.

She saw that hardness back in his eyes as dismissively she rose from the table. He hadn't liked her contemptuous rejection of what hadn't been a proposal anyway, she saw, but she was past caring what he liked or disliked.

She carried her plate to the sink, an uncomfortable silence stretching, so much so that when she turned back to the table to clear the rest of the things away, she felt compelled to look at him.

Her eyes met his, but instead of the hardness she expected to see still there, she saw that hardness had gone, that his expression had lightened. And as she watched, mystified at the complexity of the man, slowly he raised his hand and rubbed it over the fine stubble on his chin. When he did have something to say, it had nothing at all to do with his amazement that he had thought she might be angling for him to marry her—or that she had let him know just how highly she valued that particular idea.

'Might I enquire if this establishment runs to supplying unexpected guests with the use of a razor?' he enquired pleasantly.

Not knowing why, Mercy felt the strangest desire to laugh. Sternly she repressed the inclination, realising that he was showing an unexpected politeness since he must have seen her razor when he had gone looking for the aspirin.

'Sorry it's not the cut-throat sort,' she replied, keeping her face straight, 'but feel free.'

His laugh as he vacated the kitchen showed that she had unintentionally restored his good humour. And, when she realised she quite liked the sound of his laugh, Mercy no longer felt like laughing herself. What, for heaven's sake had she got to laugh about!

CHAPTER FOUR

By the time Mercy had completed the washing up, her spirits were at a lower ebb than ever. Wiping the dishes hadn't taken more than a few minutes, but in those minutes, lightning flashes of memory had visited. Memory of Philip's face when quietly he had come into her bedroom. Oh, how could she have hurt him so?

Unhappy with the picture that wouldn't leave, she tried to turn her thoughts away from Philip. But humiliating thoughts of being at the centre of village scandalmongering were not more comfortable companions. She switched her thoughts to Croft Latimer. To think that she . . .

Hastily she turned her mind away from that too, a feeling of desperation coming that nothing her thoughts touched on was easy to live with.

She searched for something she could feel better about, and found it in the knowledge that as soon as Croft had washed and shaved, he would be on his way, and that would be the last of him. Well thank goodness for that, she thought. But she was soon back again to wondering how on earth she had been able to do what she had done, when apart from knowing his name, and the fact that he ran a company just about everybody had heard of, that was all she did know about him.

Plagued by thoughts she couldn't dispel, she forced her mind away from the previous day's events, and sighed, only to discover that Philip's stricken face was back with her.

She was entirely unaware that Croft, his ablutions finished, had come to stand in the kitchen doorway, his eyes taking in the sadness of her expression.

A faint sound drew her eyes to the door. Her expression did not brighten when she saw him standing there.

'Don't . . .' he said, but left it there, as though he thought he might regret what he had been going to say. He moved from the doorway to stand close by her. Then looking down into her eyes, he said, 'He'll be back,' and sounded just as though he believed it.

So he'd guessed Philip had been in her mind! She moved a few steps away, lowering her eyes so that Croft shouldn't see into them. She knew darn well Philip wouldn't be back. What man would when he had witnessed what Philip had witnessed? And anyway, she didn't want to discuss it with Croft. He was dressed now as he had been yesterday, his suit of a superb cut.

'You'll forgive me for not seeing you to the door,' she said. Having fed the brute—even if it had been he who had cooked the meal—having given him the use of her bathroom, she did not see any reason now why he should hang about.

'Your charm doesn't match your beauty,' he murmured lightly, a none too subtle hint that she was sadly lacking in the manners department.

Oddly enough, his remark made her colour. That was before annoyance spurted that her upbringing should cause her a twinge of conscience at her ungracious manner. Good grief, what else did he expect!

'On second thoughts,' she said, 'perhaps I will show you the way out.' She offered a stiff insincere smile with her comment, as she moved past him and into the sitting room.

She was level with one of her easy chairs when she turned to check that he was following. She was fairly tall herself, but there was no way she was going to move a man of his size, if he wasn't in a mind to move himself.

He was following her, she was thankful to see, but

when she stopped, he stopped too. And it was then, having looked forward to having nothing more to say to him, that curiosity stirred in her to know just why he had been at Hilary's wedding. To know just why Hilary had been so scared. As things had turned out, it was her view that she was more than owed an explanation.

Not moving another step, and since Hilary wasn't there to ask, she saw no reason to stifle the impulse to ask *him* for her explanation.

'Why did you attend the wedding?' she asked point-blank. It had been all too plain yesterday that he hadn't been overjoyed to be there.

Her question made him raise an enquiring eyebrow. 'You sound puzzled?'

Mercy, determined that she wasn't going to be fobbed off by evasion, found a chair behind her and sat herself down on the arm. When he followed suit and took the arm of the chair facing her, she hoped it was because he too thought she had a right to an explanation.

'You said yesterday that you were not a friend of Hilary's, that you had only ever seen her once before.' None of it was any clearer today than it had been yesterday. 'Apart from that,' she confessed, 'I haven't a clue why Hilary should delegate me to . . .' She stopped, loyalty to her friend, though she must be miles away by now, making her wary.

But she soon discovered that what Croft Latimer didn't know, he had more than enough nous to guess at.

'You have no idea why she should delegate you to prevent my having a word with Giles Norman?'

She shook her head. A scene was what Hilary had been terrified of. His having a 'word' with Giles was putting it far too mildly.

'I thought at first you might have been a—good

friend of Hilary's once. But, unless you fell in love with her at first sight, then . . .'

'My first sight of that bitch was more than enough to put me off her sort for life,' he interrupted her tersely, his eyes hard, the way he said it leaving her in no doubt that far from having fallen in love with Hilary at their one and only meeting, he had taken an instant dislike to her.

'But—why attend her wedding?' she asked, still groping in the dark. 'You didn't get to have a "word" with Giles,' she added, reflecting that Croft Latimer appeared to her to be a man who, once he had made up his mind to do something, would let nothing swerve him from his course. 'And you were there for the whole of the reception.'

His severe expression faded. 'I was, wasn't I!' he said. He relented on seeing she was remembering too, and was not at ease with that remembrance. But he quickly removed her discomfiture, giving her a fresh surprise by saying, 'The only reason I went to that church yesterday, was because if I hadn't gone, then my sister Diane would have attended.'

'Your sister!'

He nodded. 'Diane Goodwin,' he said, and questioned, his eyes watching her, 'Does the name Goodwin mean anything to you?'

She thought for a moment, then shook her head. 'There's a Mrs Goodwin in the village who crochets beauti . . .'

'Your friend had never mentioned any of her lovers by name?'

'Lovers!' she exclaimed, the way he said it making it seem that Hilary had a whole string of them. 'I hadn't seen her in ages—we were at school together. It was a surprise to me when she asked me to be one of her bridesmaids. . . .'

She broke off, realising she was prattling on. Then, at

what he had said, his mention of his sister, the name Goodwin almost in the same breath as he'd spoken of Hilary's lovers, a shaft of daylight began to penetrate what had been growing more and more confusing, though she accepted she could still be wrong.

'Are you saying,' she plunged, 'that Hilary had an affair with your sister's husband?'

'It was more than that. She lived with him for a year.'

'Lived with him!'

'Does that shock you?'

With his eyes steady on her, she had little time to consider her answer. 'No, not really, I don't think. It's happening all the time, isn't it?' she said slowly. 'It's just that I never thought of Hilary—living with someone she wasn't married to.' Her voice had tailed off, but to show him she was as modern-thinking as the next girl, confidently she said, 'Your sister was divorced from her husband at the time, of course.'

'No,' he retorted shortly. 'Diane didn't so much as know he was running two homes until that bitch came and demanded she divorce her husband, to let her have him full time.'

'He was living with your sister while at the same time . . .' she gasped, knowing that *that* kind of modern thinking would never be hers.

'He has the sort of job that frequently takes him away,' Croft told her heavily. 'She was used to him being away for weeks at a time. It never entered her head to question his absences.'

'That's terrible!' she exclaimed, nowhere near to coming to terms with what she was learning about Hilary, who must, by the sound of it, have known her lover Goodwin was deceiving his wife. Trying hard to get over what, after all, had been a shock, Mercy thought then she had the answer to everything.

'Your sister was going to come yesterday to ruin

Hilary's wedding—her marriage—the way Hilary had ruined hers?' she questioned.

Croft shook his head. Seeing she was floundering, he told her concisely, 'I'd been to see Goodwin.' He left her to imagine what had gone on, nothing very pleasant by that hardness that was back in his eyes. 'Your—friend—was there. On my advice Diane threw him out. But she says she still loves him, and with Goodwin now wanting to come back, she wanted to witness for herself that—that woman—is finally out of her hair—his life.'

'Oh,' said Mercy, and, sure she now had it right, 'But you told her you would come and witness for her?'

'Diane's been through enough without having to degrade herself by breathing the same air as her husband's former mistress,' he said shortly.

She silently agreed with him. But thought then, having received the explanation she had been after, that there was nothing more to say.

'Hilary obviously recognised you from that visit you made to the home she shared with your brother-in-law,' she concluded. 'And was terrified in case you told Giles she had made a good stab at wrecking your sister's marriage.'

But she was to learn it wasn't the end, as Croft soon put her right about the sordid truth that Hilary had been afraid Giles would hear.

'I told you Goodwin was frequently away on business. Your friend isn't the kind of woman to put up with that for long. The reason she was throwing a fit when she collared you to be photographed with her, was because she was afraid I would tell the man she had been able to ensnare into marriage, that at the time he was paying court to her, probably sleeping with her too,' he said bluntly, 'with her type of morals she wouldn't see anything wrong in it—she was still living with—in every sense of the word—my sister's husband.'

Nausea hit Mercy then. Hilary had been a live wire at

school, but their fun had always been innocent fun. Would she have gone the same way had not her father put his foot down about her going off to London with Hilary when they'd both been seventeen?

Instinctively she knew that she would not. Perhaps she would have been wiser than she was now, but never could she see herself acting in such a disgraceful fashion. The word disgrace brought back guilt at her own shortcomings, guilt at her unfaithfulness to Philip.

'But you didn't tell Giles any of this,' she said, wanting hurriedly to leave her thoughts.

'Even with you sticking to me like a second skin,' he said sardonically, watching the colour of fresh guilt break in her pale face, 'I don't doubt I could have found the opportunity.'

'But you didn't,' she persisted, having been more than paid back, in her opinion, for having pretended she fancied him.

Suddenly, when she had thought there was dislike only in her soul for Croft Latimer, he showed himself up as human. Mockery went from him, and Mercy found herself near to liking him, as he confessed:

'One glimpse of the besotted look on Giles Norman's face for his bride was enough to tell me that where she was the sort who would bounce right back again—he was the one who would suffer for a long time to come.'

For seconds after he had finished, she just sat and looked at him, the first genuine signs of friendliness coming to her eyes. And as Croft looked back, a smile started to break in him. But all at once she was remembering that he had made love to her when she had been in no condition to stop him, and she was back to not feeling friendly to him at all.

Abruptly she stood up, her eyes going to the door, to the way out. 'Thank you for explaining all this to me,' she said, knowing his smile would have faded, knowing he was far too astute not to guess at the thought that had settled on her. 'But with Hilary and Giles now safely airborne there's no need for me to detain you any longer.'

He was there with her at the door when she reached it, a hardness in him as cuttingly he enquired, 'Duty done?' And she blanched when, sardonic again, he asked, 'Tell me, Mercy, are you always *so* loyal to your friends?'

At innuendo he was a past master, she thought, and coloured again, hating that she did so. What more proof could he want that he could easily cut her down to size?

'I didn't mean to—go as far as I did,' she replied stiffly, her hand going to the door handle. Then she let her hand fall from the handle as the thought came, to hell with it; and looking him squarely in the eye, she told him, 'I was wrong to pretend I fancied you when I didn't.' And faltering only slightly, 'But you have been—more than recompensed for that.' Pink lit her cheeks again as she hastened to stammer, 'I didn't mean—mean last ni . . . I mean that—that I shall have to stay in Ravensmere . . .'

'And face the storm of gossip?'

'Yes,' she said, grateful that he had understood what she had really meant.

He came to her side, his hand going to the handle of the door, ready himself now to bid his adieu. 'It won't be more than a nine days' wonder,' he said laconically, the door handle already beginning to turn.

'You don't know Ravensmere,' she muttered disconsolately, and walked away from the door, only to find he hadn't gone. He was still there; it was his turn to hesitate, before, after several moments' thought, he brought out:

'Look, if it's any help—if things get too bad—I have a cottage a few hours' run from here. You're welcome to use it as a bolt hole till it all blows over.'

He sounded sincere. And the idea had definite appeal. She would never live down what had happened, she knew that, but if she took herself off, away from the wagging tongues, say, for a couple of weeks, then surely at the end of that time the first flames of the fire would be over. But did she want to run away? Was it right that she should? Wasn't it moral cowardice to leave them to get on with it?

Her indecision must have shown, she realised, though it was without pressing her in any way that Croft said, 'I've had the cottage for some months now, and though I can't promise you luxury, I think you'll find it has everything you require. Plus,' he added, 'the advantage of being able to hide yourself away until the new school term starts.'

It hadn't been in her mind to take up his offer for more than a couple of weeks. But she was beginning to feel pulled to taking him up on it. None of the plans she and Philip had made for their holiday would come to fruition now, time was going to hang heavily on her hands. And it wasn't as though she could afford to go anywhere else.

'You might find the place a little untidy when you get there,' Croft said in semi-apology, obviously taking it from the way her eyes were showing an interest that she had accepted.

'Untidy?' she queried, a warning bell going off in her head.

'I didn't find time to clear up after the last . . .'

'You use the place?' she shot at him, suspicion rearing its head.

'That *was* the point of buying it,' he said, loftily she thought. 'I need a hideaway too sometimes, somewhere I can unwind, relax.'

Unwind! Relax! Oh she'd been right to take heed of that warning bell, she thought. Work hard he must to lead the conglomerate of companies he did. And there must be times he needed to retreat from the pressures involved. But she saw at once what his game was—and she had nearly fallen for it!

'Thank you so much for your kind offer, Mr Latimer,' she said, sarcasm oozing, careless of the slight frown that came to him as her tone registered. 'You'll forgive me if I turn your offer down, I hope,' she added. Then anger taking her, she was spitting, 'But *one* night spent with you is more than enough to last me a lifetime.'

His brow cleared. Slow on the uptake he wasn't. And there was mockery in his voice as he hit back with, 'That's what they all say.'

Swollen-headed swine, she thought, and turned her back on him. She'd be glad when he had gone. She knew she wouldn't begin to get her thoughts into any sort of order until that door had closed behind him.

But hearing no sound, the door remaining unopened, she had to turn round, if only to satisfy herself what he was doing. He had taken a business card from his wallet, she saw, and was scribbling something on it. She remained where she was as he came over and handed the card to her.

'There are two telephone numbers there,' he said, his voice even now, serious. 'My office and my home. If you change your mind, give me a ring.' And not waiting for her to tell him he could keep his phone numbers, still serious, he said, 'I shall be too busy to use the cottage for a while—it could do with someone there to give it an airing.'

Mercy drew a relieved breath the moment Croft Latimer had gone. Oh, how nearly she had been taken in! She dropped the card he had given her on the low table, not bothering to so much as look at it. He must have thought she had hatched out of her shell yesterday, she mused. And at that notion, that that was more or less what she had done, a whole flock of thoughts swooped in to keep her in torment.

Hastily, as though to outstrip her thoughts with the speed with which she worked, Mercy got busy trying to occupy herself. Then, the kitchen immaculate, the sitting room, already tidy, came in for the same treatment.

But it was on going into her bedroom, ready to attack it, that she caught sight of the bridesmaid's dress she had worn yesterday, which must have been placed on a chair, but had slithered to the floor, and disgust with herself took her.

Never wanting to see the offending dress again, she picked it up and bundled it into a paper bag ready for the dustbin. How could she have done what she had?

Her thoughts were many and varied that day. When she wasn't being disgusted with herself, or despairing of the days she had to live through before it started to get better, a picture of Philip would present itself. And if it wasn't her ex-fiancé's face she saw, then a mental image of Croft Latimer would appear, and she would see him again, his face serious as he told her, 'I shall be too busy to use the cottage—it could do with an airing.'

That Sunday seemed to her to go on forever. She could have shortened it by going out, she knew that. However, the only place she needed to go was to the Drivers' house to pick up her car and the clothes she had changed out of.

But it wasn't only because she didn't want to meet anybody who would try and ferret out all they could, that she didn't want to go for her car that day. Justin Driver had a severe ticking off coming to him; if he'd been anywhere as near grown up as he liked to believe, had he not so childishly mixed tasteless vodka with innocuous drinks before handing them to her, none of this would have happened. And she knew that if he was around when she went, not only would she be having a few short and sharp words with him, but that if it ended up with him giving her a mouthful of cheek, she might very well let herself down and try her hand at boxing his ears.

By the time she went to bed, Mercy felt emotionally drained. She had gone over and over everything in her mind to the point of exhaustion, but still her thoughts couldn't find rest. That Hilary wasn't coming out of this smelling of roses, was something she'd had to accept too. All she hoped was that she had meant it when she had declared she loved Giles. She didn't want to think that she had married Giles purely for his 'gold-lined wallet'. Croft had noted too that Giles was extremely vulnerable where Hilary was concerned.

As vulnerable as Diane, his sister, must be about her husband, she thought. Diane's faith must have been shattered anyway, if she was waiting for her husband's mistress to be safely married before she would think of taking him back. Not only that, but needing to have Hilary's marriage witnessed before she would believe it was true.

Of course, that telephone call of Croft's made sense now. It must have been his sister he was telephoning. 'He's all yours if you want him,' he had said. Unquestionably he had been referring to Diane's husband. And the 'Yes—she did' must obviously be the answer to the question 'Did she get married?'

Mercy's last waking memory, before sleep eventually claimed her, was of being taken to task by Croft for her lack of manners. 'Your charm doesn't match your beauty,' he had said. Did that mean Croft Latimer thought she was beautiful? Her eyelids stayed down—as if she cared, she thought—she went to sleep.

Determined not to invent excuses to become a hermit, Mercy left her flat the next morning. She didn't stay waiting for her ground floor landlady to unbolt her door when she heard the locks rattling as she passed by. Miss Sefton not only had a safety chain on her door, but kept her door locked and bolted at all times, and knowing that Miss Sefton only ever went out when she had to, Mercy also knew that her landlady was an avid telephone conversationalist. The lines had had twenty-four hours to start buzzing.

But having escaped by the skin of her teeth from anything the prim Miss Sefton had to say, she found she was not so lucky when she turned into the main street.

Her heart sank as she saw Mrs Vialls, who appeared to have taken root, in earnest conversation with Mrs James who had been at the wedding on Saturday. She didn't need to stretch her mind too far to know whom they were taking to pieces.

'We were just talking about you,' Mrs Vialls confirmed before Mercy, not giving in to the impulse to cross the street, could get past.

'Good morning, ladies,' she said brightly, determined not to be drawn, and hoping to be allowed to slip away.

'Mrs James was just saying how you appeared to be having a fine time at Hilary Driver's wedding,' said Mrs Vialls before this aim could be achieved.

'I think all the guests had a good time,' she said, as pleasantly as her gloomy spirits would allow.

'Some more than others,' was the rapid come-back.

'It's usually the way,' answered Mercy, stepping off the pavement, the only way to get round. 'Must dash,' she said, already on her way. 'Have masses to do today.'

She strode on, knowing full well she had just supplied fuel for further speculation. Apart from picking up her car, she hadn't a thing to do that day. Which, with Mrs Vialls knowing practically everything there was to know about everybody's activities, she probably knew too, and was most likely now wildly speculating on what it was that kept Mercy so busy.

She was stopped twice more before she made it to the Drivers'. Once by a Mrs Foster who lived near to Philip and his mother. But she had seen her in advance, and again used the excuse of having a lot to do for saying, 'Can't stop,' and hurrying on.

However, it was when she met Kathleen Etheridge, a girl she had been briefly friendly with before Kathleen had got herself a steady boy-friend who took up most of her time, that her ploy of being rushed off her feet came unstuck.

'Hey,' said Kathleen, looking disposed for a long chat, 'what's this I hear about you and Philip Bailey splitting?'

So the news was out. Her footsteps halted. She was at a loss to know what to say. She could hardly say it was a mutual thing, she thought rapidly. Yet pride made her reluctant to admit that Philip had thrown her over—wild horses wouldn't have made her say why.

'News travels fast,' she said, avoiding any admission that would soon get back to Philip.

'You know Ravensmere,' said Kathleen with a grimace. 'You can't keep anything quiet around here. There's a regular gas-bags' convention going on in the post office.'

Inwardly Mercy groaned, making a mental note to steer clear of the post office. 'Who'd live anywhere else?' she said.

'Try me,' Kathleen replied, rolling her eyes. 'Tell you what though, Mercy, if you want to sue a few for slander, you can call me as a witness.' She went on to reveal the worst as far as Mercy was concerned. 'They're saying you got sloshed at Hilary Driver's wedding, and were half carried out by some stuck-up London bloke.'

'Well, at least while they're talking about me, they're leaving someone else alone,' Mercy managed, her last hopes shattered. Then, trying to overcome the knowledge that her worst fears had been realised, 'I must go, Kathleen, I've got to pick up my car from the Drivers'.'

As soon as the words were out, she knew she had slipped up. Kathleen's face took on that same expression she had seen on Mrs Foster's, that expression of wanting to hear it all at first hand.

'This chap from London did take you home from the wedding, then?' she questioned cunningly.

With the knowledge that the game was up, her only defence was to brave it out. 'Well, somebody had to,' she admitted.

'So long as he didn't have his wicked way with you,' Kathleen quipped, half in fun, half waiting for any juicy tit-bit.

And it was then that pride came and shoved Mercy's dignity up on to a high horse. 'Good heavens, Kathleen,' she said, offended, 'What on earth do you think I am?'

She didn't regret her implied lie as, without bumping into anyone else, she made it to the sanctuary of the Drivers' home. She wasn't sorry either that no one apart from Mrs Tandy, busy with polish and a duster, was at home.

'Hello, Mercy,' she said. 'Come for your clothes? Everybody's out. I've put them in a plastic bag for you.'

'Hilary and Giles go off all right?' she asked, following Mrs Tandy along the hall, thinking to head her off before she too started asking pointed questions.

'Yes, thank goodness. That Hilary was only here for two nights, but what with clearing up after her and trying to get the place looking ship-shape after the wedding, I'm only thankful it wasn't any longer.'

Mrs Tandy would have gone on interminably, and since talk was being kept away from herself, Mercy could have let her. But the plastic carrier now in her hands, she was ready to escape while Mrs Tandy still had 'that Hilary', and the way she left the bathroom, as her subject.

'I'll have to go,' she smiled, edging towards the door.

But she hadn't escaped before the cleaning lady got in with:

'I hear you and Philip Bailey nearly came to blows.'

'Nearly came to blows!' she repeated, startled.

'Word had it that you had a fight over that man who took you home,' said Mrs Tandy, muttering to herself, 'I never did find out who he was,' before she went on to advise, 'Though if you've fallen out because that London fella took a shine to you, then I wouldn't lose any sleep over it.' And while Mercy was realising that inventive tongues had wasted no time, she heard Mrs Tandy go on to air the view, 'That Philip Bailey was never meant for you. He's . . .'

What Philip was, Mercy didn't stay to find out. Though as she took herself off for a drive and drew her car into a lay-by some miles from Ravensmere, of all she had heard that morning, it was Mrs Tandy's words that came back to her time and time again.

She and Philip had been admirably suited, she had thought. They never rowed, or had a cross word. Why, even when he had come into her bedroom yesterday, Philip hadn't blazed at her, or attempted to punch Croft Latimer on the jaw as . . . She stopped her thoughts right there, the loyalty she still felt to her ex-fiancé threatened at the thought that started to rear that she would have thought more of him if he had gone for Croft.

But Philip wasn't like that, she mentally defended him. It was because he wasn't aggressive, like her father, that she loved him. Not that she loved him because he was such a welcome change from her stern parent, she thought hastily; then saw that what with one thing and another, her thinking was all over the place.

One very clear fact stood out, though. She wasn't Ravensmere's favourite person at the moment. Oh, if only she could get away for a few days. Not that it would stop tongues from wagging. But at least she wouldn't be around to be got at.

Having already rejected Croft Latimer's offer of the use of his cottage, Mercy gave only brief thought to using one of the two telephone numbers he had given her. She couldn't remember where she had put his card, anyway.

If she hadn't left herself only enough to get through on until next pay day, the rest of her money given to Philip to put in their joint savings account, she could have afforded to slip away until the gossip had cooled, she mused. She started up her car. It was getting on for teatime, she had missed her lunch. She'd better get back and make a scratch meal out of something. Perhaps she would write to her parents, it didn't matter that she was due a letter from them, her mother was always pleased to hear from her. She could write a chatty letter about Hilary's wedding, though she knew before she set pen to paper 'that Croft Latimer's name wouldn't be mentioned.

Parking her car in the spot she always did outside Miss Sefton's house, Mercy opened the front door and was just congratulating herself that she hadn't been waylaid by a soul, when, closing the door behind her, she was confronted by the scrawny figure of her vinegary landlady.

'Hello, Miss Sefton,' she forced cheerfully, well knowing that since Miss Sefton never came out from behind her locked door unless it was essential, their meeting in the hall was not accidental.

'I would like a few words with you, Miss Yeomans,' said Miss Sefton, a lady who seldom smiled, and who was certainly not smiling now.

Miss Yeomans! That in itself told Mercy she was out of her good books, if she had ever been in them. She had always been Mercy to everyone, and that included her landlady.

'Certainly,' she said, unable to hold on to her cheerful manner, not looking forward at all to the pending interview in Miss Sefton's dark, dour sitting room.

'It won't take long,' Miss Sefton told her, a clear indication that what she had to say could be said there in the hall.

Not that that worried Mercy unduly. The telephone wires had obviously been busy and the hall seemed to be neutral territory. If she went into Miss Sefton's apartments, she would be the one to be making excuses to get out again, since clearly Miss Sefton wanted information about what had happened between her and Philip.

'If it's about Philip Bailey and me,' Mercy said, bringing it into the open, and just a teeny bit fed up, for all her loyalty to Philip, in being at the sticky end of it all, 'then,' she smiled to take the edge off her words, 'you'll forgive me, Miss Sefton, but I would much rather not discuss it.'

She thought she had delivered that politely and without causing too much offence. But on seeing her landlady's uncharitable face tighten, a spite in her eyes she had never before noticed, she realised she had not taken kindly to being told what her tenant wanted. And there was nothing but venom in the prim spinster's voice when she flapped her starched body and shocked Mercy into staring at her in disbelief when she told her what *she* wanted.

'I object very strongly,' she told her in no uncertain tones, 'to having a gentleman's car parked outside my house all night.' And while Mercy had never given a thought to where Croft had parked his car, Miss Sefton was saying viperishly: 'I am not going to stand for such goings on in my house. I never have, nor do I intend, ever, to run a house of ill repute. You will oblige me, Miss Yeomans, by vacating the upstairs flat at the earliest possible moment.'

And as Mercy stared thunderstruck after her, not believing what she had heard, Miss Sefton marched to her own flat. The next sounds to be heard were the rattling of the chain and the door being bolted—sounds telling her that the interview was at an end.

CHAPTER FIVE

STILL stunned, Mercy automaticaly found the key under the plant pot. She let herself into the flat she had just been told to vacate, the words she had heard spinning round in her head. The meal she had been going to prepare was nowhere in her mind as she sank down into a chair.

This development was something she had not so much as considered! Yet, on thinking about it, thinking of the prudish Miss Sefton, she saw too late that it was something she should have foreseen.

Would it have made any difference if instead of shooting off that morning she had stayed when she'd heard her landlady unlocking her door? Perhaps Miss Sefton would have been more amenable then, she thought futilely. Instead she had hurried off, and for her sins left Miss Sefton to seethe all day, to wind herself up, so that having delivered her speech, she hadn't even stayed around to hear Mercy's defence.

But what defence had she? The evidence of Croft Latimer's car outside was all Miss Sefton needed, apparently, to know he had stayed all night. And though Mercy objected strongly to being accused of turning the house into a house of ill repute, that, in the dried-up old spinster's eyes, was clearly how she would see it.

Her mind as busy as last night it had been, as evening approached, Mercy saw she was at the cross-roads in her life. At the cross-roads, yet with no idea which direction to take. All she knew was that now more than ever she needed to get away. She needed to think. Needed somewhere where she had peace and quiet.

Needed to be where she didn't have a resentful landlady under her feet.

She needed to be away from a place where every time she went out into the street she ran the risk of being accosted by someone wanting a supplement to the latest. She didn't doubt that on Miss Sefton's next trip to the post office to collect her pension, she would be telling one and all she had given Mercy Yeomans her marching orders. Thank goodness her rent was paid four-weekly in advance, she had some time to go yet.

Again she thought of the money she had jointly with Philip. They were both signatories, so either of them could draw on the account. The only trouble was, Philip held the savings book, and she was loath to see him to ask him for it.

Poor Philip, she thought, he would hate it too, to be the centre of gossip. She wasn't doing him any favour either by staying around to keep the pot boiling, was she? She hadn't doubted that her engagement was at an end. Philip's silence confirmed it. He could have come round yesterday, could have telephoned, had it been in his mind to look for extenuating circumstances.

It was an hour later, still not knowing which way to turn, that Mercy finally allowed in the thought that had been nudging at her for some time but had been pushed away as unthinkable before it could properly settle. Croft Latimer had an empty cottage doing nothing— why was she hesitating?

The thought that Philip too would benefit if she removed herself for a few days, gave her the push she needed. Mercy hesitated no longer. She set to searching until she found the card Croft had given her; it was on the kitchen windowsill. She must have been going to throw it in the bin but had got side-tracked, she thought.

Not sure what she was going to say to him if he was in, she dialled his home number. She had time only for one controlling breath before she spoke to the man she had yesterday thought never to hear again, as almost instantly the phone was picked up.

But it was not Croft's voice that she heard. A sultry, totally feminine voice answered, 'Hello,' and gave the number she had dialled, so she knew that it wasn't a wrong number. And at that moment, Mercy took heart. For clearly, if Croft was entertaining Miss Sultry Voice, any fears she had about the wisdom of what she was doing must be groundless.

'Can I speak with Mr Latimer?' she asked.

'Who's calling?' came back a voice that sounded more snappy than sultry on hearing it was a female at the other end.

But before she could tell the woman her name, she heard Croft's voice, impatient, as if he wasn't too pleased about a telephone interruption.

'Latimer,' he announced himself.

'It's—Mercy Yeomans here,' she said, tension in her suddenly at the thought she didn't want, but which had just come, that he might not have been serious with his offer yesterday, although he had appeared so at the time.

'And what can I do for you, Mercy Yeomans?' he enquired, good humour in his voice, his impatience gone.

'Well . . .' she said, a clear image of him in her mind as she crossed her fingers and hoped he wasn't one of those people who said things without meaning them. 'Well, I was wondering—if you're not using your cottage yourself,' she gabbled quickly, 'if, well, if you'd allow me to use it for a few days?'

'As bad as that, is it?' he queried.

'Things aren't—too good,' she understated. And heard she could uncross her fingers, when he straightaway said:

'I'll put a key in the post to you.'

But grateful as she was, she needed to be away now and not have to wait for any foul-up in the mailing system. She felt she just had to be away the next day.

'Er—isn't there any other way of me getting in without waiting for the post?' she asked hopefully.

Silence was her answer, so that though she hadn't heard the phone go down, for a moment she thought he had assumed there was nothing more to say and had hung up.

But he was still there, humour in him too, as he said, 'I don't leave a key beneath a flower pot.' More seriously he added, 'It's that urgent?'

'I . . .' she said, and knew he would never understand even if she did start to tell him. 'I'm a bit mixed up right now,' she confessed. 'You intimated you found peace and quiet at your cottage. I have a few things to think over.'

'Bailey?'

She wasn't quite sure what he meant by bringing Philip's name into it. But she answered him as best she could. 'Things are over between Philip and me. But since the fault is in no way his, I think he would feel a shade better about it if I removed myself for a short time.'

'And what about your feelings?'

What about her feelings? Was he asking how she felt not to be engaged to Philip any more? It was only then that she realised she hadn't got around to thinking how exactly she did feel that she was no longer to marry Philip.

'I—don't know,' she said, and truthful though that comment was, she was strangely bewildered that she shouldn't know.

'Have you a pen handy?' Croft's question brought her back from her speculations.

'Yes,' she said.

'Then take down this address,' he instructed. And on

learning she would be driving to the village of Abbeybridge where his cottage was, he further instructed her on the best route to take, ending with, 'I'll see there's a key there for you tomorrow.'

'Tomorrow!' she exclaimed. And as a feeling of being wary started to creep in as she analysed that if he wasn't intending to post the key, then somehow or other he must be going to have it delivered, she couldn't hold back the question, 'You—won't be there, will you?'

She didn't get to hear his reply, for the sultry-voiced female she had completely forgotten while they had been talking, suddenly said—which must mean she was very near to him for her to have heard, 'Darling— you're not cheating on me, are you?'

Mercy put down the phone. Croft hadn't answered her. But he had no need to. From the sound of it, his time was more than fully occupied.

Having packed her case the night before, with all she thought she would require for the few days away, Mercy was up early and anxious to be off before Ravensmere was astir on Tuesday.

Feeling like a criminal she went quietly past Miss Sefton's door, and was in her car and leaving the village behind before it dawned on her that she stood to arrive at the cottage long before the key had turned up.

Thoughts that there was a possibility that Croft might be the one to deliver the key, regardless of her hopes the night before that he would send someone else, bred in her a great reluctance to see him again.

Was it so strange to feel that reluctance, she pondered, as spotting a general store on her way, she pulled up and shopped for the few supplies she would need to last her. Her first encounter with him had shown it would have been better never to have tangled with him. Not that anything of that nature was likely to happen again, ever, she'd take jolly good care of that. But even so, that reluctance to see him would not go away.

She stopped again before her journey was completed, purely to kill time. But, after what seemed an age, but still had a few minutes to go to the hour, she came to the conclusion she might as well get on. Croft would be hard at work in his office by now, she was sure. He wouldn't have taken time off to deliver the key personally she thought, deriding herself and her nerves for her idiocy.

Lupin Cottage, she discovered when at last she found it, was in an isolated spot tucked away from the sleepy village of Abbeybridge. The village itself was nowhere near the size of Ravensmere, little more than a few farm cottages with one solitary store on the end of a terrace of four.

Leaving her things in the car, no other car in sight, she stood admiring the charm of what looked to be a two-up-two-down dwelling. With a bit of attention given to the garden which looked as though it hadn't been weeded this summer, a bit of elbow grease on the windows, she could be happy there, she thought.

Though since she was only here for a few days, she had better get going and see if the key had arrived yet.

She went up the path, wondering where whoever delivered the key would have put it. Surely not in the keyhole, she thought, and was nearing the front door when the corners of her mouth picked up, and a gurgle of laughter, alien to her just recently, had to be emitted. For there on the step, hidden from view by a shrub that grew in front of it, was a florist's paper wrapping, which on closer inspection she saw was covering a flowering geranium.

Unhesitatingly Mercy bent to lift the flower-pot, and just as unhesitatingly, her fingers picked up the key which she had known would be underneath.

She went inside, and it was as if the laughter that had broken from her when she had seen that florist's wrapped flowerpot had released her from the depression that had been with her since Sunday.

She was soon at work putting the cottage to rights. As Croft had said, it was untidy. She even found she was humming, as, the sun now off the windows, she set herself the task of getting them to shine. And throughout that day, the serious thinking she was there to do never touched her.

An unearned happiness that she knew she had no right to feel, wakened with her the next morning. Sun streaming through the window set her smiling and getting out of bed.

There being no bathroom, though thank goodness there was a flush toilet out in the yard, Mercy washed in the kitchen, and put her guilty happiness down to the fact that she was away from Ravensmere, away from scurrilous tongues.

It was so peaceful there at Lupin Cottage that a sort of serenity washed over her, making it impossible for her to get started on any sort of thinking that would have destroyed her peace of mind again.

Having cooked herself a three-course lunch, Mercy thought some exercise was called for. There wasn't a tin of polish to be found in the place. Not that she could for a minute see Croft spending the time he had in his hideaway polishing furniture. But a dab of it here and there wouldn't come amiss, she thought, so, as a means of getting the exercise she needed, she set off to the village for the purchase.

Her route to the store had been a direct one. But, a tin of polish in her shoulder bag, she detoured on her way home, cutting across a field resplendent with buttercups, some of which she picked to further brighten up her temporary abode.

By the time she was ready to return, she had amassed other wild flowers, and some twigs. And by good fortune, having not seen a flower vase at the cottage, she had come across an old pot, someone had dumped in a hedge, its glazing cracked, but which would wash up very nicely, and be just the thing for her wild bouquet.

Humming softly as the cottage came into view, she slowed her footsteps as she made out that a car was parked right behind her saloon. Her humming came to an abrupt end, her first thought being that Croft was her visitor. But as she made out that the car was not the Mercedes, she was able to settle also that the unexpected adrenalin that had pumped through her veins was merely instinct getting her ready to square up to him, since she didn't want him there.

She had reached the car, a smart sports model, though with the top on in spite of its being such a sunny day, when its blonde occupant, obviously seeing her from the rear view mirror, emerged. And proved to be very far from male.

Superciliously, was the only word that fitted the way the fashionably turned out female looked her over, Mercy thought. Cold blue eyes inspected her from top to toe, then went disdainfully from her to the pretty yellow heads of the buttercups she had collected.

'So you're Mercy Yeomans,' she drawled in a voice Mercy had no trouble in recognising as one she had heard before, recently.

'That's right,' she replied, disliking the other girl before they went further, as she wondered how she managed to walk on those higher-than-high heels. But even while recognising the voice as that of the female who had asked Croft 'Darling—you're not cheating on me, are you?' she couldn't do anything about the devil in her that chose that moment to surface. 'You have the advantage of me,' she said, her lips wanting to twitch as she recalled those were almost the first words Croft had used to her. 'Croft didn't tell me your name.'

She didn't like that, Mercy could see, as the sulky mouth went down. 'He's discussed me with you!' she snapped nastily, looking her over again, as if she couldn't believe that Croft, even holding back on her name, would ever discuss her with the little nonentity with her washed-out frock, and with a face that hadn't seen so much as a powder puff all day.

Having thought it had gone on for long enough, and not wishing to hurt anyone's feelings, even if the other girl did look as if she had a swinging brick for a heart, Mercy was just about to come clean. But when she looked at those hard blue eyes again, all of what she had been going to say deserted her. For the superior astonishment there, as though to say she simply couldn't believe Croft knew her, much less had had a conversation with her, instantly put her back up. For days now she had been running around with her tail between her legs; in her view it had gone on for quite long enough.

She adopted a superior look of her own, hoping it outmatched that of the condescending blonde, then tossed the question back at her.

'Croft discuss you with me!' she said, injecting into her exclamation a surprise of her own that she should suppose they had any time for anyone but their two selves. 'Hardly,' she scoffed.

Mercy didn't like at all the stabbing glare that flashed from those cold eyes. Though she did give the girl top marks for retaining her cool, even if she did find the question that dripped from those brilliantly painted lips offensive, as, bluntly contemptuous, she said:

'You're surely not trying to make me believe you have been to bed with him!'

This kind of talk might be normal in the blonde's set, Mercy thought, but it had never been in hers, and she could not help the fiery blush that came to give her away. Indeed everything about her gave away what she would never have admitted. It was there in the way she lowered her eyes for a moment before she raised them to see the blonde was looking flabbergasted at what she had to believe.

'You have!' she said, clearly shattered. 'He's . . .'

Mercy didn't let her finish. She didn't know what the girl was doing there, and didn't much care. Before her arrival she had felt near to being serene. This high and mighty creature had ruined all that.

'You may be used to this sort of conversation,' she interrupted, finding that when it came to being blunt she wasn't at the back of the queue herself, 'but I am not. And I've got much better things to do with my day than to get into a discussion with you on whom I sleep with.' And with that devil in her again, urging her on, her pride pricked to be looked down on as something an angler would usually bait his hook with, she added, 'But if you haven't got that far with him yet, I'll tell you this for nothing, Croft Latimer is a great lover.'

With that, Mercy marched up the garden path and went indoors. And it wasn't until long after her blonde visitor had gone that the heat went out of her, and she thought, Oh my, was that me out there! But she had to allow herself a chuckle at the memory.

It was not till later, having used her tin of polish to satisfaction, having put her buttercup bouquet in the sitting room window, and washed her hair, that Mercy began to wonder what had got into her.

Last night she had gone out like a light, but when she lay in bed that night, she was to find that sleep was very far away.

For hour after hour she lay sleepless, and it wasn't the noises of the country that kept her awake, she knew that. She was used to hearing the screech of the owl, the bark of a fox. Had she really told that haughty blonde that if she hadn't got that far with him yet, Croft Latimer was a great lover!

For a while, she dropped off into a light sleep. But soon she was awake again. Awake, and her first thought was, of course he had got that far with the blonde. It was obvious, since she had turned up at his hideaway, that she had been there before. And one only had to look at her, the same type as Hilary and her loose-talking friends, to know that *she* wasn't averse to helping him relax.

Her mind was still too full of Croft Latimer and his line in mistresses to admit one tiny thought of Philip or what she should be thinking about, her future, when, as dawn began to break, she settled down for some sound sleep.

The day was well under way when she awoke. And even though it was way past the time she usually woke up, she had a feeling she wouldn't have woken then, had not some sound in the room disturbed her.

Her eyes darted round the room. Then she was struggling to sit up, struggling to wake up. For surely she must still be asleep, must be asleep and dreaming!

But as her open eyes opened further in amazement, stayed open to stare witlessly at the tall, broad-shouldered figure standing at the bottom of her bed, Mercy, her mouth going dry, knew that she wasn't dreaming. For the apparition spoke:

'Good morning, Mercy,' it said. 'So I'm a great lover, am I?'

'I . . .' was as far as her dry throat would allow. And she had nothing to add when she could speak. For she was discerning that Croft Latimer didn't look at all pleased to have received her opinion on him as a lover through the auspices of the blonde. 'She . . .' she tried, grasping for some form of defence.

'She,' he said grittily, 'happens to be Felicia Woodward, a very distressed lady who called at my apartment to tell me . . .'

'She didn't waste any time, did she?' Mercy got in, coming rapidly to life, and not liking the tale-bearing blonde any better this morning than she had yesterday. 'I didn't ask her to come here looking down her nose at me as if I was something crawly that had just been scraped off a mouldy piece of bacon . . .'

Her voice faded as he moved and came to stand at the side of the bed, to look down at her with hard grey eyes. She felt shrivelled at the burning light that suddenly came to those eyes. But she was nowhere near to backing down, when after a moment's thought, he rapped sharply:

'Are you aware of what you have done?'

She was all too well aware of what she had done. She had sent his lady friend away with a flea in her ear, and she still couldn't regret it.

'If you didn't want me to tell tales out of school, you should have ensured she kept away from Lupin Cottage,' she snapped. 'I didn't want that sort of a conversation,' she pointed out, annoyed that he had probably fussed over the snooty Felicia, while she always ended up being put in the wrong. And, angry with herself to think she was bothered by anything he did, she said defiantly, 'I'd had enough of going around hiding my head in my collar. She started it, I didn't.'

She hitched over a few inches when he lowered himself to sit on the edge of her bed. It was three-quarters size and, near to the other edge, she was about to tell him that anything he had to say to her on the subject of Miss Felicia Woodward could be said downstairs, when he got in first.

'You realise, of course, that you have ruined any chance of my getting engaged to Felicia?'

'You were going to . . .' she began, heat going out of her. That was before the thought returned that she had had enough of being everyone's rubbing rag. And anger was there again as she flared, 'Well, it just serves you right.' And remembering his role in her engagement's ending, she added, 'That's exactly what you did to my engagement, more or less.'

The heat had gone from her again, but as she saw

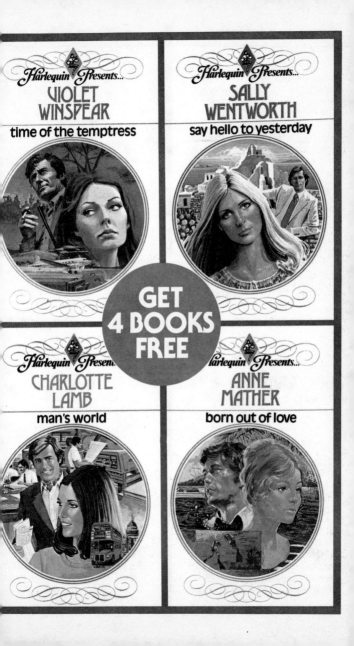

Harlequin Presents...
VIOLET WINSPEAR
time of the temptress

Harlequin Presents...
SALLY WENTWORTH
say hello to yesterday

GET 4 BOOKS FREE

Harlequin Presents...
CHARLOTTE LAMB
man's world

Harlequin Presents...
ANNE MATHER
born out of love

Say Hello to Yesterday
Holly Weston had done it all alone.

She had raised her small son and worked her way up to features writer for a major newspaper. Still the bitterness of the the past seven years lingered.

She had been very young when she married Nick Falconer—but old enough to lose her heart completely when he left. Despite her success in her new life, her old one haunted her.

But it was over and done with—until an assignment in Greece brought her face to face with Nick, and all she was trying to forget. . . .

Time of the Temptre
The game must be played his way!

Rebellion against a cushioned, controlled life had landed Eve Tarrant in Africa. Now only the tough mercenary Wade O'Mar stood between her and possib death in the wild, revolution-to jungle.

But the real danger was Wode himself—he had made Eve aware of herself as a woman.

"I saved your neck, so you feel you owe me something," Wad said. "But you don't owe me a thing, Eve. Get away from me. She knew she could make him lose his head if she tried. But the wouldn't solve anything. . . .

Your Romantic Adventure Starts Here.

Born Out of Love
It had to be coincidence!

Charlotte stared at the man through a mist of confusion. It was Logan. An older Logan, of course, but unmistakably the man who had ravaged her emotions and then abandoned her all those years ago.

She ought to feel angry. She ought to feel resentful and cheated. Instead, she was apprehensive—terrified at the complications he could create.

"We are not through, Charlotte," he told her flatly. "I sometimes think we haven't even begun."

Man's World
Kate was finished with love for good.

Kate's new boss, features edito Eliot Holman, might have deva tating charms—but Kate couldr care less, even if it was obvious that he was interested in her.

Everyone, including Eliot, thoug Kate was grieving over the loss her husband, Toby. She kept it c carefully guarded secret just ho cruelly Toby had treated her ar how terrified she was of trusting men again.

But Eliot refused to leave her alone, which only served to inf ate her. He was no different fro any other man. . . or was he?

These FOUR free Harlequin Presents novels allow you to enter the world of romance, love and desire. As a member of the Harlequin Home Subscription Plan, you can continue to experience all the moods of love. You'll be inspired by moments so real...so moving...you won't want them to end. So start your own Harlequin Presents adventure by returning the reply card below. <u>DO IT TODAY!</u>

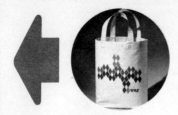

Business Reply Mail
No Postage Stamp Necessary
if Mailed in Canada

Postage will be paid by

Harlequin Reader Service
649 Ontario Street
Stratford, Ontario

N5A 9Z9

Canada Post
Postes Canada
021

Croft look at her and observe her blush, she wished that she could sustain that anger. For the grim expression he had worn throughout had gone, and suddenly his eyes were no longer hard. They were looking at her with a softer light she found confusing, as he asked:

'Broken-hearted, Mercy?'

'Oh—how do I know?' she said, feeling wretched all at once. 'I came here to get things clear in my mind, but I'm as confused as ever I was.'

His arm came about her shoulders with a touch of sympathy that surprised her. 'Don't, Croft,' she said, trying to shrug his arm away. But she chose just that moment to turn her face to his, and then discovered that his face was much too close.

But it was when Croft left his arm where it was, the feel of it burning into her thin covering, that Mercy realised that she had never known what confusion was until this moment—she was actually quivering with it. For the strangest thing was that, far from wanting him to take his arm away, suddenly it came to her that she wanted it there, exactly where it was.

'Croft,' bewildered, she whispered his name. And it was as if he knew all about this new confusion that was inside her, for understandingly he smiled, and, tenderly, he placed his mouth over hers.

When he broke his kiss Mercy knew she should pull away, pull away from his arms, for both arms were around her now. But she didn't pull away. And she had no idea why she did not move. Dumbly, as if in shock, she just sat there and looked at him. Though she wasn't in shock, she thought, bemused. That kiss had seemed so natural somehow.

She wasn't shocked either, when traces of a smile hovered on Croft's mouth the moment before he kissed her a second time. A kiss that was nothing like the first, a kiss that had her knowing she should be doing something other than putting her arms around him, had her knowing that she shouldn't be holding on to him when he drew her close and she felt his body heat through the thin shirt he wore.

With his third kiss she felt a new sensation—a sensation of quivering anticipation as his hands began to glide over her spine. And she definitely knew she should be doing something other than clinging to him when his hands moved to caress her breasts. But alarm signals were totally ignored as his kiss deepened. The feel of his mouth on hers she found electrifying, and she could do nothing to break away.

She wanted him to kiss her again, she discovered, when his lips moved from hers to whisper light kisses across her throat and to the swell of her breasts. But it was then that she discovered in herself something that nature had kept well hidden until that moment. That magical something that set her hands moving, touching him. That magic that had her wanting to feel his skin against hers. That something that caused her trembling fingers to move to the buttons on his shirt.

Kiss after kiss she gave him. Having no protest to make when with a groan that told her he had that same need that she had, in one movement he had slipped her nightdress from her shoulders and was pressing his bared chest against her, was pressing her back against the pillows. And for Mercy, all of it was magical, a magic shared with Croft such as she had never shared with Philip—though Philip was far from her thoughts then.

'Croft.' She whispered his name as she saw a fire burning in his eyes as he took the bed covers from her and lay down with her.

She knew then what was going to happen. And wanted it to happen. Knew just then when his mouth feathered kisses down to her pink-tipped breast, one hand cupping the creamy swell, that for both of them there was no going back. It had happened before, she knew that, but without memory of that first time they had made love, she felt nerves pick at her as his love-making became more intimate.

'Croft,' she said jerkily, the feel of his caressing hand on her smooth belly almost too much.

'What is it, my dear?' he breathed, his voice thick, but his consideration for her not lost although she could see an inferno of desire in his eyes.

She knew her cheeks were scarlet, but with nothing secret between them, she made herself look into those burning eyes.

'Nothing,' she said chokily. But when, while he still looked at her his hand began to renew its caressing, the words came, jerkily again. 'I know—I-I've been—this way before—but it's all new to me—I-I can't remember.'

As she stammered to an end, she thought for one awful moment that she saw the flame in him dip. And she knew panic that perhaps that other time hadn't been so good for him. Perhaps he was having second thoughts about this time. And the aching need he had aroused in her was swamping any thought but that she just could not bear it if he left her like this.

'Love me,' she whispered urgently, her trembling fingers on his hair-roughened chest. Croft raised his chest from her, and in panic she was again pleading, 'Love me.' She didn't want the magic to end there, could not bear that it should. 'I want you, Croft,' she cried, even as her cheeks burned with her confession.

She saw his glance move to take in the sight of her uncovered breasts. Saw the flame of desire sparking there in his eyes. Then his eyes were leaving her breasts, but the flame still blazed when he looked at her, his hand coming to the side of her face, his voice carrying that same emotion of wanting as he murmured softly:

'This time will be a time for you to remember.'

Her mouth curved into a gentle, giving smile. 'Yes,'

she whispered back. And thinking of the first time not being too special for him, 'It will be better for you this time, won't it?'

Again she saw that flame of desire in him falter. But found she had no need to panic that he might be going to reject her. For, after a pause where he seemed to hesitate, as though picking his words, she heard him say:

'Don't—expect too much, my dear.'

Swept away on this tide of yearning new to her, Mercy had little comprehension of what he could mean. But the way he had told her not to expect too much . . . The note there, as though he was—warning her, almost, about something—left her questioning when his head came down and he would have kissed her, taken her to rediscover, perhaps to remember that time before.

'It's only the—first time that it's—er——. It's better after the first time—isn't it?'

Fresh confusion broke in on her then, for as Croft heard the innocent question, saw the innocence in her eyes, a sound came from him, a torn sound. For a long moment he looked down at her where she lay, and then, gently, he kissed her. A kiss like that first kiss he had given her, tender and without passion. But he numbed her for countless seconds, when his mouth left hers, and he said:

'Sweet Mercy—my dear—this *is* the first time for you.'

CHAPTER SIX

MERCY was too far gone in her need of him to make any sense of what Croft had just said. All she was capable of at first was of lying there and staring up at him.

Even when the words 'This *is* the first time for you' did start to make sense, she could not believe he was meaning what he seemed to be saying. And she just had to question:

'You mean—you and I have never . . .'

'Never,' he said, his face unsmiling as, still partly over her, he confirmed what she thought he meant.

But having been taken to a precipice in his love-making, even then, the depth of her confusion was too deep for her to accept what it was he was saying.

'But you stayed the night in my flat,' she said, shaking her head, struggling for comprehension. 'You were in my bed when I woke up. You said . . .' She broke off, unable to remember then what he had said.

'I came to your bed because after trying to get comfortable in a chair that had never been designed for anyone over six feet to sleep in, it seemed the logical thing to do. You were using only half the bed,' he said, his voice even and soothing, 'and I had received a very clear impression I had been invited to the other half.'

Almost trance-like, she asked the question, 'You intended to stay the night?'

'When you passed out cold, I thought I'd better. I couldn't shake off a doubt that crept in that you might not have asked that young man to lace your drinks—that doubt that maybe you weren't used to knocking it back. There was a chance you could have woken up ill, needing someone there to get you to the bathroom.'

All the time he had been speaking, the chaos in Mercy's mind and emotions began sorting itself out. Slowly she had been coming down from that glorious peak of wanting he had taken her to. So that by the time he had finished telling her he had stayed, but only to push her into the bathroom if she had woken up vomiting, she was in a state of not caring for his thoughtfulness. She had, in fact, come down from one peak, only to go furiously storming up another.

'*Get away from me!*' she exploded, when having done away with explanations Croft looked as though he was about to gently kiss her again. 'You swine!' she shrieked, pushing at him with all her strength as she yelled, 'You unmitigated swine!'

Successfully she managed to dislodge him. But only to be made more furious by the cool way he sat on the edge of her bed and began rebuttoning the shirt she had so eagerly unbuttoned. Hot colour scorched her that nothing had happened between them on the night of Hilary's wedding, but that not too many minutes ago, it very well could have done. And not only that, but that she had *wanted* it to happen.

It was of no help to see him stand, far more in control than she was, to see him casually put his hands in his pockets as he looked at her and remarked:

'Don't take it too badly, Mercy . . .'

'Not take it too badly!' she shouted, colour of shame on her when she followed his eyes and saw him looking at the naked front of her. 'Get out!' she screamed, hastily grabbing at the covers and hugging them to her. In her fury she wanted to hurl herself at him and claw at him, but in her state of undress, modesty belatedly arrived to temper the need to scratch his eyes out.

'Am I to take it you no longer want me to—love you?'

If only she had something to throw at him! She hated

him. Hated him that he could throw that back at her. 'Go away—I destest you,' she spat at him. And when he still hadn't gone, but stood watching the colour freely ebbing and flowing in her face as each remembrance of how easily he had got to her, flitted in before being driven away, she grasped at what dignity she could muster, and told him with seething dislike, 'I want to get dressed.'

'Perhaps you'll have cooled down when you join me downstairs,' he suggested, managing to look so innocent of crime that it was a wonder to her that he didn't sprout wings.

She stayed in bed only a moment after he had uncaringly strolled out. And though she loathed to dress without first seeing soap and water, she decided that there were some occasions in life when the niceties of civilisation had to be done away with, and that this was one of them.

And not only did she dress, but snatching down her suitcase from the top of the wardrobe, she raced to fill it. Her stay at Lupin Cottage was over.

Mercy was still seething, though emotional tears were not very far away, when she snapped the locks of her suitcase shut, and marched down the stairs.

She unlatched the door at the bottom of the stairs, and, intending never to say another word to Croft Latimer, she went sailing through the sitting room. But her purpose to sail straight out through the front door was fustrated.

Oh, she had seen him in the sitting room all right. She realised when he came out from the kitchen that he must have heard the stairs door. He had guessed what she was about—and had moved speedily to prevent it.

For by the time she got to the outer door, it was to find he was there barring the way. And he was getting in first, before she could tell him to let her pass, his voice sarcastic so that had not his words brought her up

short, it would have been quite possible that she would
have attempted to belabour him with her suitcase.

'Off to tell dear Philip the good news?' he drawled.

'Ph . . .' Good heavens! She hadn't given Philip a
thought since . . .

'You remember Philip,' prompted Croft, a pleased
wickedness entering his eyes as he read in hers that
Philip hadn't surfaced in her mind at all that morning.
'He's the man you used to be engaged to.' All sign of
pleasure departed, though his voice still held mockery,
as he added, 'He's going to be delighted to hear you are
still as virgin now as in all the time of your engagement
he let you remain, isn't he?'

'Shut up,' Mercy snapped, having had enough of his
baiting before he got started. Then she saw there wasn't
a trace of mockery about him either, as sharply he bit
back:

'Are you also going to tell him that if I hadn't let out
the truth a while back, you would, right now, be
without that virginity?'

'Will you let me pass?' she said, throwing him a look
of hearty dislike. She could do without reminders of
that sort.

'He's not the man for you,' said Croft, not budging,
reminding her that Mrs Tandy had said much the same
thing. Though unlike Mrs Tandy, who wasn't privy to
such things, he went on, 'You have fire in your blood,
Mercy. A fire that should be met with fire. You need a
man who . . .'

'Shut—up,' said Mercy distinctly with emphasis. And
seeing that, short of driving a hole right through him,
she was never going to get to her car, she let her case
fall from her fingers, hoping it would land on his foot.
Though since he didn't cry out as she turned about and
went to the kitchen, she doubted that it had.

She could have tried to make it through the back
door, she supposed, as she washed her hands, cut a slice

of bread and popped it under the grill. But with him playing some game (she hoped he would soon get tired of it) of keeping her prisoner, she didn't want a tussle with him, those knowing hands on her body if he tried to prevent her leaving that way. Besides which, she thought, she had left her case in the sitting room.

'We share the same habits, I see.' She ignored him. 'You never go anywhere without breakfast either,' he continued, causing her to wish she had never got started on toasting bread. 'Add a couple more pieces to that, would you?' he requested pleasantly, coming away from the doorway and going to fill the kettle. And conversationally excusing that he too was hungry, 'I left home early this morning.'

Silence reigned in the kitchen. He can cut his own bread, she thought mutinously, toast his own toast. But when from the corner of her eye she saw he was getting two cups out, she realised that having shown him she was far from being a child, it was suddenly ridiculous to start behaving childishly. She cut two more slices from the loaf, but was careful not to catch his eyes as she pulled out the grill pan.

Having been spitting mad with him, having thought that fury would never die, now that Croft had changed from being a sarcastic mocking person to a man who seemed to understand that she didn't want to talk, some of her rage ebbed. He had made no attempt to press her into conversation as he put two cups of coffee on the table. Had not said another word as he rooted round for the butter and marmalade, then went to the cutlery drawer.

He had been wrong to go on letting her think what she had, she thought, taking a place at the table. Even if he had been set on getting his own back for the way she had pretended to be bowled over by him at Hilary's wedding, he was wrong. Especially was he wrong, her thoughts went on, as, her appetite strangely unaffected, she silently munched toast, when he knew that because of him her engagement was broken.

'Could you pass the marmalade, please?'

Her eyes flicked to find the marmalade near to her plate. Unspeaking she passed it over, and went back to her thoughts. Yes, he was the swine she had called him. And yet, her brow puckered, there must be something in him that said he wasn't all that much of a swine. He had got her just where he wanted her. Could have taken her—she hadn't been resisting—far from it, she thought, pink in her face flaring. And yet, when many men would have taken what was being offered—she cringed to recall she had all but begged him to take her—Croft had chosen just that moment to tell her the truth about the night they had spent in the same bed.

'Mercy.' She looked up. 'Don't,' he said.

Unaware that he had been watching her for some minutes, she saw that his face was solemn, sincere. 'Don't?' she queried.

'If you've been having a private post mortem—don't,' he explained. 'You're a warm, responsive woman. What happened between us, my reaction to you—your reaction to me—it was a natural happening given the circumstances in which it was set.'

'I've—never—been like that before,' she said, a feeling in her that he should know she didn't go around flinging herself at any man who kissed her. A feeling in her that he should know it shamed her that she had pleaded for him to love her.

'If I didn't know that before,' he said, and smiled gently so that all traces of fury left her, 'then the way you've been changing colour these past five minutes would have told me you have been in agony with remembering it all.'

Swiftly then, and with an ease that helped her to put aside her embarrassment, Croft was taking her with him into a different conversation, that soon drove mortifying thoughts from her mind.

'Tell me how you like the cottage?' he asked. 'You found your way here without too much trouble?' And before she could answer either question, 'Fancy more coffee?'

She admitted she wouldn't mind another cup. Slightly amazed, for her father had never poured himself a cup of coffee in his life, and Philip too was not averse to being waited on, Mercy saw Croft leave his chair and rinse out their coffee cups while the kettle boiled.

Seated again, fresh coffee to the right of both of them, she saw that Croft's questions had not been merely idle ones to get them off a subject she was obviously not happy with.

'How do you like Abbeybridge?' he asked.

'It's quieter than Ravensmere, but what I have seen of it, I like very much.'

'Not too quiet for you?'

'Oh no,' she said straight away, 'I love it. Love the solitude.'

Oddly, the silence that followed while they both imbibed coffee, did not seem uncomfortable. It was on the way to being a companionable silence, she thought. Which was odder than ever. For striking sparks off each other as they frequently appeared to, theirs, she thought, was not a relationship where a companionable feeling should enter so easily.

'You said you had some thinking to do,' he said, reminding her of her telephone call to him. 'Has it been quiet enough for you to come to terms with your— problems?'

She returned her cup to her saucer, wondering if he was referring to any one particular problem. Was he still of the opinion that Philip would 'soon be back'? About to reiterate what she had said before, that she knew things were over between her and Philip, suddenly she realised that she didn't want Philip to want her back! That she *didn't* want to marry Philip!

She lowered her eyes to her cup. Croft Latimer was sharp. She didn't want him reading that shock in her eyes that came with her new knowledge. Knowledge there was no time then to set about analysing.

'My—problems will still be there when I get back to Ravensmere,' she said, realising she hadn't answered him.

'But you're going to tell Bailey I didn't . . .'

'I wasn't referring to Philip,' she cut in quickly. And as anxious to be off the subject of Philip as she was to be off the other subject Croft didn't find any difficulty in discussing, she opted to tell him the only other thing that popped into her head. 'I've had notice to quit my flat.'

That he hadn't expected to hear anything like that, was obvious by the slight raising of his brows. 'Because of the gossip that's circulating in Ravensmere?' he asked. The way his mouth twitched, though he tried to control it, showed that he wasn't taking it seriously, as he added, 'I'm sure your landlord will rescind your notice once word gets around that you and I didn't . . .'

'Landlady,' Mercy cut in again, beginning to wonder if any conversation between them could be had without *that* cropping up. 'Miss Sefton is my landlady, and . . . and it won't matter a button what she hears to the contrary,' not that she could see herself lowering herself to tell anybody anything, she thought, pride rearing. 'She's the main reason I telephoned you on Monday. I'd had it up to here with everybody poking and prying into my business too. You're labelled the "stuck-up London bloke", by the way.'

'Nice,' he remarked. And she forgot where she was for a moment when he laughed, the laugh she had liked, evidently not a scrap put out at his label.

'Anyway,' she resumed, sure she must be mistaken that she liked his laugh, 'I had just got in on Monday after taking myself off for a few hours, when Miss

Sefton waylaid me in the hall—she lives in the flat below,' she explained. 'Not to put too fine a point on it, she objected to your car being parked outside her house all night, and would I leave at the earliest possible moment.'

A dullness of spirit entered her as she came to an end. She was no longer looking at Croft. But if he burst out laughing at what he considered some small-minded villager getting all bitter and twisted, then she wasn't so sure that her coffee dregs wouldn't go flying across the table.

'Would you like me to go and see her?'

The enquiry came evenly, and surprised her by sounding serious. She raised her head to look at him. He *was* serious, she saw. But she shook her head.

'No. No thanks,' she replied. 'It wouldn't do any good. One car outside her house all night that wasn't mine, was sufficient for Miss Sefton to believe everyone thinks she's running a house of ill repute.'

'Is that what she said?'

His face had fallen into stern lines. He looked tough, she thought, and could imagine Miss Sefton having an attack of the vapours if he arrived on her doorstep looking like that.

'It doesn't matter,' she said, her pride rising again. 'Besides, I wouldn't want to stay there. I'm—I'm not sure I haven't had it with Ravensmere anyway!'

'But your job's there. You love village life.'

Yes, he was right, she did love village life, she thought, not knowing how the change in her had come about, when at seventeen it had seemed a cruel blow that her father would not let her go to the big city to live. Perhaps he had known her better than she knew herself.

'One village is much the same as another,' she said, and found suddenly that she was speaking her thoughts aloud. 'There's always talk in any small community. I expect every village has its equivalent of Miss Sefton too,' she said. And owning she felt more mixed up than ever, she came out with what all at once seemed to be clearer than anything else. 'As for my job, I'm not sure a change wouldn't do me some good. I can do secretarial work anywhere.' She lapsed into silence, then said, 'I'll have another coffee, then be on my way.'

Having felt flat, she felt her own lips twitch at the automatic way Croft passed his cup over for a refill as she stood up. But, her back to him as she reheated the kettle, her smile fell away when she heard him say:

'You don't have to go, you know, Mercy.'

His words brought her spinning round, a wary look in her eyes. He was showing her a bland front, but even not knowing what he was suggesting, she didn't trust him. And she didn't hesitate to bluntly set about finding out.

'Dim, I don't think I am,' she said, switching off the kettle as it boiled. 'But can you throw a little light on that remark?'

'Bring the coffee over and I'll explain,' he said, and had nothing more to say until she was again seated opposite him. Then he began, 'We could help each other on this one.' Which did nothing to remove that look of suspicion in her eyes.

He had desired her, had Croft Latimer. If he was about to suggest . . . Her fingers tightened on the handle of her coffee cup. He'd noticed, she realised, when he suddenly sent her a grin of some charm.

'Relax lovely girl,' he said. 'I assure you I am not suggesting anything in any way destined to earn me a shower of hot coffee.'

That so nearly teased out a matching grin, that Mercy did relax, though she was hard put to keep her features as bland as his had been.

'Exactly what are you suggesting?' she enquired quietly, her fingers coming away from her cup.

'As I see it,' he began again, 'you still haven't sorted yourself out. It appears to me you require far longer than a couple of days to get things straight.'

That was true enough. The fog she was in never looked like lifting. 'You're suggesting I extend my stay?' She was wary again. She didn't want to return to Ravensmere yet, if at all, but how did her staying at Lupin Cottage help him?

'What a suspicious madam you are,' he said, reading her look easily. Then, getting down to brass tacks, he told her: 'It has not gone unnoticed by me that there has been something of a transformation about this place since I was last here.'

Transformation! All she had done was clean it up a bit. True, it shone everywhere; windows, woodwork, and the splash of the red geranium, the yellow buttercups, all helped to brighten it up, she supposed.

'You like the buttercups?' she asked, and found herself smiling when he did. Though she was sure it couldn't be because he had liked them, where his girl-friend had looked down her nose at them.

'I like them,' he said. 'But what I'm getting at, is that this place looks homely, lived in. It needs a woman's touch.' She wasn't with him, and it showed. 'What I'm asking,' he said, 'is this. Will you, Mercy Yeomans, kindly consider staying on here,' and at that mistrustful look she instantly shot at him, he added, 'as my caretaker.'

'Caretaker!' she exclaimed. Oh, wasn't that a new name for it!

'Why not?' he asked, before she could explode. 'You said yourself you'd had it with your job.' Had she said that? And before she could get round to remembering what it was she had said, 'The cottage needs living in—and you do like living here, don't you?'

'Er—yes,' she said, thinking that before meeting him she had usually known her own mind, but since then, it

seemed to her she had been nothing but confused. He
was looking sincere about his offer, she noted. She
decided that for the moment, until she discovered
differently, she might as well play along with him.

'You are offering me a job,' she said thoughtfully.
'You're saying that you will be my employer?'

'The cottage needs somebody living here full time,' he
replied. 'I haven't yet found time to get round to
carrying out any of the alterations I had in mind when I
bought it.'

Being tucked away from anywhere as the cottage
was, his words made her stray from the point to ask on
impulse. 'How on earth did you get to hear it was up
for sale?'

'Diana lives a few miles up the road. Knowing I was
looking for a hideway, she tipped me off.' And while
she was recalling that Diana was his sister, that
indirectly it was through her that she and Croft had
met, he went on to say, 'If you stayed on, you could
have all the time you need to sort yourself out. You'd
have a job. Be living in a village. A village you have
said you like,' he reminded.

Unaware her guard had slipped, Mercy thought, yes,
she did like the village. Love the spot where he had his
cottage. But—caretaker?

Realising she was getting to like the idea—she
definitely felt a pull to spend some more time in Lupin
Cottage—she saw she had better start putting up some
opposition to the plan before the idea took root and
became difficult to discard.

'It—wouldn't be permanent,' she said, her mind
settling on the practical one of her lack of resources. 'I
would have to get some other job. I mean, it's not as if
secretarial posts are plentiful in all villages, is it?'

'Naturally I'd pay you a caretaking fee,' he said
promptly, having no trouble in reading from what she
said that money had to be a consideration. 'You

would live here rent free, of course,' he further tempted.

Get thee behind me, Satan, Mercy thought. And came up then with what was a very big 'but' in what seemed an ideal arrangement.

'What about you?' she asked cautiously. 'The cottage would be lived in, the way you want it. But—this place is your hideaway. That's the only reason you own it. You would be here too occasionally, I imagine?'

Her question didn't perplex him, as he easily replied, with a throwaway carelessness, 'I'd give you a key to your bedroom—if that's what is worrying you.'

Worrying her! Never would she forget the feeling he had aroused in her that morning—nor her response to him. And never must she get herself into such a position again.

'And its duplicate?' she pressed.

'To be honest with you,' said Croft, ignoring her question as though not thinking it worthy of an answer, 'the only time I come down here is when I feel the stress of my job becoming too much.' Her eyes shot to him. Were caught and held, as he underlined his meaning. 'This is where I retreat when I need a rest from both mental—and physical—activity.'

Clearly he was telling her that the next time he arrived, there would be no thought in his head for a repeat performance of what had taken place that morning. But looking at him, Mercy saw he looked as strong as a horse and virile with it. He looked as if he had an inexhaustible supply of strength, she thought, unable to lose a niggling doubt that he was very gently leading her up the garden path.

And then she looked at his eyes. Eyes that had lost their hardness, but eyes, she suddenly observed, that were showing signs of strain—showing signs of the pressures he must work under. He looked in need of a rest, she thought. And it was then as she looked at him,

that her sensitivities were attacked and doubt vanished.
Those were lines of tiredness around his eyes, she was
sure, and everything else went out of her head, as quite
without thinking, she asked:

'Is that why you came today, because you felt the
need to rest?'

As soon as the words were out she was recalling what
he had said when he first arrived. She knew why he had
come and it wasn't so that he could unwind. He had
come to sort her out for what she had said to the girl he
had hoped to marry. And while not liking Felicia
Woodward any more now than she had done before,
her sensitivities were still under attack, and she was
again the warm-hearted girl she had ever been.

'I'm sorry. Of course that wasn't your reason,' she
said in a rush. 'And I'm sorry for what I said to Miss
Woodward. Truly I am. I didn't mean to mess things up
for you when—when I told her what I did.'

She went a faint pink at the knowledge she now had
but hadn't had before, that Croft Latimer certainly
knew how to make love to a girl—he'd had her a willing
instrument in his arms without too much trouble,
hadn't he?

Aware of how easily Croft spotted her changing
colour, how easily he could come up with the reason for
it—though this time he made no comment, seeming to
be quite happy to sit there watching her trying to
extricate herself from the tangle of her emotions—she
was again rushing in.

'If you'll give me her phone number, I'll—I'll ring her
and explain . . .'

She stopped. What on earth was she getting all
stewed up about? And angry suddenly, with him as
much as herself, for he had been quite happy to let her
go gibbering on, she let that anger flare into life as
abruptly she changed tack, and challenged:

'Why didn't you tell her yourself that we hadn't . . .'

Her short burst of anger fizzled out. 'That you hadn't . . .'

She saw his smile as she couldn't finish. Heard his voice, pleasant when it came and he took pity on her. 'Perhaps I didn't love her as much as I thought I did,' he said. And he appeared to be so unconcerned by a door being slammed on his matrimonial hopes with Felicia Woodward, that he took time out to take a glance at his wrist-watch. And was then exclaiming, 'Ye gods, is that the time!'

He was then, all at once, the business man she guessed he was when seated behind his desk. And his voice was brusque, that of her prospective employer, as he said:

'I have to put some time in at my office today. Tell me now, Mercy Yeomans—do I have myself a caretaker or not?'

About to tell him 'Not', Mercy opened her mouth. Whether he read from her expression what her answer was to be, she didn't know. But his brusque manner fell from him, and suddenly a smile of such great charm winged from him to her, that just as suddenly, she was powerless to deny the appeal of the little boy in him when, sinking her with his winning smile, he said:

'Please.'

'Oh, all right,' she heard herself say begrudgingly.

And when she had nothing to laugh at, suddenly her musical laugh sounded in the kitchen. Croft's baritone laugh joined it.

CHAPTER SEVEN

CROFT LATIMER was a past master at getting his own way, Mercy thought the following morning. Though why he should be the first person she should think of when she awoke she didn't know. It could be because she still wasn't easy in her mind about the size of the cheque he had given her before he left, she mused.

A month's caretaking fee, he had called it, brushing aside her statement that she was used to being paid in arrear, not in advance, and proclaiming when she had protested about the amount, 'I'm used to paying for the best'. A statement that had taken her aback when she realised it was a sort of compliment. By the time she had been ready to protest again, Croft was at the door, another flicked glance to his watch telling her he had more important matters to be getting on with than a time-wasting argument.

And she had important matters to deal with that day, Mercy thought, getting out of bed and going downstairs to wash. Quite when she had got around to 'sorting herself out,' she couldn't have said. But by the time she had gone to bed, she had come out of the numbness of shock that had gripped her since waking on Sunday morning, and knew she had been right when she had declared she thought she had finished with Ravensmere.

It had been her own feeling of humiliation, the fact of Philip finding her like that, of the whole village knowing about it, that had set her running. But away from Ravensmere, perhaps because she was armed now with the knowledge that Croft had let out that it was not as it had appeared to Philip—would have appeared to anyone—a return to Ravensmere held none of the nightmares for her it might have done. And to return was what she would have to do; if only to pick up her personal belongings and arrange for her furniture to be put into store.

She had last night written out her resignation ready to post this morning. Her new job with Croft as her employer wasn't to be a permanent one, as she had told him, but at least she was assured of a roof over her head for a while. She would get round to thinking about her future in due time. For the moment, her first priority was to get her past dealt with.

Wanting her visit to Ravensmere over and done with, by half-past eight she was heading her car in that direction. Today, not bothered about anyone else she might bump into, she only hoped that she wouldn't bump into Philip.

She had been shaken to know that she no longer wanted to marry him. Had thought about that realisation long and hard once Croft had left, but only to be shaken once again when she began to see quite clearly why she didn't want to marry Philip. She was not in love with him. Oh, she still loved him. He would most likely always have a place in her affections; for what had happened had not changed him from being the dear kind considerate person he had always been; but she just wasn't *in love* with him.

More delving had shown her that Philip wasn't in love with her either. But if he hadn't discovered that yet, then she did not wish to see him and open up a wound that hadn't had time to heal over.

'Morning, Mrs Vialls,' she called to the woman she had a few days ago dreaded seeing, and who was on street patrol when she parked her car outside Miss Sefton's house. Not giving her a chance to get a word in, she went on, 'Lovely day, isn't it? I see you have a new hat—it suits you.' And while Mrs Vialls, halted in her stride, put up a preening hand to her new head adornment, Mercy left her standing and went indoors.

Clearing out her flat, ringing the storage people an
the various services, took longer than she ha
anticipated. She guessed Miss Sefton would come out t
see what was going on if she didn't go to tell her. S
after a trip down to her car with her first suitcase ful
Mercy thought she might as well tell her now.

She knocked at her door and waited while the bolt
rattled. Then with a pleasant smile, she was facing th
acidulous lady, and telling her:

'I'm moving out today, Miss Sefton. I'll let you hav
the key to my flat and its spare before I go.' And befor
Miss Sefton, who was looking not very pleased to find
far from timid tenant standing there, could issue an
vitriol from her pursed lips, she went on, 'I'm afraid th
storage people can't get here until Friday. I'll com
back if you would rather, bu⁺ . .'

Miss Sefton could not, as Mercy suspected, wait t
see the back of her. 'I'll let them in,' she said tightly, he
thin mouth working in corrugated lines.

'Thank you, Miss Sefton, that's more than good o
you.' Mercy was on her way back upstairs when Mis
Sefton called after her.

'I hope you intend leaving a forwarding addres
There will be bills coming in for your telephone and th
electricity you have used.'

Having been in touch with both authorities, lettin
them know where to send their account, Mercy saw re
at the implication that she was doing a moonlight fli
She checked her anger. Miss Sefton wasn't th
pleasantest of people, but she was old, and that alon
decreed that one shouldn't let fly at her. Someone ha
obviously got it wrong somewhere in the genera
thinking that with advancing years all women, eve
those who could not have been very nice in their youth
should overnight suddenly turn into sweet old ladies.

'I'll let you have my new address before I leave,' sh
said as evenly as she could manage.

A feeling akin to happiness came over her as the dust of Ravensmere fell from her departing car wheels. Or was it relief that she had seen nothing of Philip? she wondered. She had been afraid that might happen when, needs must, she had nipped to the villages' part-time bank to change Croft's cheque. Was it relief from avoiding such an encounter that gave her this glow inside, she pondered? Or was it that she felt happy just to be going back to dear little Lupin Cottage? Oh, what the heck did it matter what it was, she thought, she had posted her letter off to the school, and all she could think of now was that she was free! Free!

She spent the next morning in finding a home for the things she had collected the day before. She had brought with her several flower vases. But on changing the water in her buttercup and twig arrangement, she decided she liked the country look of them in their cracked, glazed pot just the way they were.

She did put a few ornaments out on display, however. And all in all, she went to bed well pleased with her efforts. To her mind, the cottage now looked like home.

On Friday morning she went to the village shop to renew her supplies, and found the lady behind the counter remembered her from her previous visit, and was in a chatty mood. Used. to village life, Mercy thought it best to let it be known, just in case Abbeybridge had the counterpart of Mrs Vialls who would invent anything she didn't know, that she was using Lupin Cottage while its owner was absent.

'Such a pretty spot up there, isn't it?' said the shopkeeper, going on as Mercy agreed, 'I did hear Mr Latimer was going to have some alterations done?'

'I think it's nice as it is,' said Mercy, not rising, and smiled good-naturedly as she went out with her carton of purchases.

Not being hungry at lunch time, loving her freedom, she decided she would eat later. Consequently the afternoon saw her in the kitchen, her hands covered in dough, the pastry for the apple pie she was making taking shape, when she heard the sound of a car pulling up.

Quieting a heart that for no reason had started to race, she went to the sitting room window to see that it wasn't Croft, as her mind had jumped to think. It wasn't Felicia Woodward's car either. Though when she saw a fair-haired female emerge, for a moment her spirits dropped, before she saw the blonde hair didn't belong to Felicia Woodward, but to some other woman she had never seen before.

Scooting back to the kitchen to wash her hands, she heard an imperious knocking on the front door before she had fully got rid of the clinging dough. Hastily she dried her hands, then went to discover who her visitor was.

She opened the door to see a thin, smartly dressed woman. She looked about thirty, Mercy saw, noting the shadows under the woman's eyes—a sign, she thought, that she had been ill, or that she was a very poor sleeper. But her manner was as imperious as her knocking, as straightaway she demanded:

'Who are you? What do you think you're doing here?'

Her tone wasn't guaranteed to bring out the best in Mercy. It instantly did away with the strain of sympathy she had felt at the woman's haggard appearance.

'I live here,' she said shortly. 'Who are you?'

'You live here!' Her question went unanswered. 'By whose authority?'

Though it did not seem to be any business of hers, there was a fair amount of confidence in the other woman's voice, enough anyway for Mercy to consider the woman must be known to Croft.

'By Mr Latimer's authority,' she said, and saw the

grey eyes of the woman widen as she gave her closer scrutiny.

'He never said . . .' he began.

Then, as if she couldn't believe it, causing Mercy to wonder if this was another of Croft's women, another he had been on the verge of proposing to, and to take a swift look down to see that her visitor's left hand was bare of any adornment, the newcomer went back to being assertive. Her manner was a shade less imperious, however, when she said:

'You have proof of this?'

'I have his phone number. You can give him a . . .'

'I know my brother's phone number . . .' the woman started to say.

But suddenly Mercy was feeling happy again, and she was exclaiming before the other could finish, 'Diane! You must be Di—Mrs Goodwin.'

'He has spoken of me?' she questioned, her haughty manner starting to subside.

Mercy's smile had started to peep out. But suddenly she was conscious that Diane Goodwin would not like it at all if she knew that Croft, not expecting they would ever meet, had told the story of her strife-torn marriage.

'He—said he had a sister called Diane Goodwin, but we . . .' she stumbled, and left it there, not realising that Diane would think, as she had implied to Felicia, that they were much too busy with themselves to let a third person in for more than a moment. 'Come in, do,' she invited, standing back. 'I'm sorry I left you standing on the step, but . . .'

'But my attitude rather put you off,' smiled Diane, stepping over the threshold, her eyes taking in the change in the sitting room from the last time she had seen it. 'I'm sorry too,' she said. Then she went on, 'When Croft said he was looking for somewhere where he could bury himself, I got a distinct feeling he meant he wanted somewhere where he could enjoy the solitude of his own company.'

'Oh,' said Mercy, pink washing her face as she saw the construction Croft's sister was putting on her being there. 'He—we . . .' She faltered, her tongue getting tied up as she tried to get out the words to say that it wasn't like that.

'Why, he even said as much.' Diane smiled as she talked over what Mercy saw *she* saw as her embarrassment. 'I was on the phone to him only last week about . . .' It was her turn to falter, 'about another matter,' she resumed, her eyes clouding, prompting Mercy to remember what that other matter had been. 'He said then that I was the only woman who knew about Lupin Cottage.'

'I—er ——.' Mercy said. She sympathised with Diane, who couldn't yet have patched it up with her husband since she wasn't wearing her wedding ring, but she could not beleive that Croft had not told Felicia about the cottage. Then her heart gave an unaccountable skip as she remembered that Felicia had been with Croft, hadn't she, when over the phone he had said exactly where Abbeybridge was and given the address. Realising that Diane was attentively waiting for her to add something to her 'I—er——', she fell back on the old, 'Would you like a cup of tea, Mrs Goodwin?'

'I'd love one,' she accepted. 'And please, call me Diane.'

And, more at ease than Mercy, she followed her into the kitchen, excusing her previous blunt manner by revealing she had taken to coming to check on the cottage when she was that way, ending:

'I thought my worst fears were justified when I saw washing on the line,' reminding Mercy her washing must be dry by now. 'I thought, oh no, squatters!'

Mercy laughed as they adjourned to the sitting room. It was over tea-cups that she determined to tell Diane that she was there as Croft's caretaker, and no more than that. She thought she had the very opportunity, when Diane asked:

'Have you known Croft long?'

'Not long,' she replied. 'We met ...' she stopped abruptly. Oh goodness, how could she tell her where they had met! '... recently,' she said, and smiled to cover that her mind was racing on.

Clearly Diane was still trying to come to terms with what her husband had done. To mention Hilary's name, reveal that she was a friend of Hilary's, would bring it all boiling to the surface, no chance of Diane trying to forget, to put it behind her and try to make a fresh start. Just one word about Hilary, she thought, and those deeply shadowed eyes would be showing tomorrow that she'd had another sleepless night.

'More tea?' she offered, noticing her guest's cup was empty.

'Please,' replied Diane. Then brought out a question that must seem natural to her, 'Is Croft coming down tonight?'

'No,' answered Mercy promptly. And so glad to have successfully skated over where she and Croft had met, she went tumbling head first straight into a hole of her own making, by drawing a relieved breath and saying blithely, 'He didn't say when he'd be coming again when he left for his office the other morning.'

That Diane had quickly adjusted to the situation she thought she had uncovered, and said nothing more than, 'Oh, I expect he will be down as soon as he can make it—you know he works all hours,' did nothing to make Mercy feel any better.

'Actually,' she said, deciding she had dithered long enough, 'I'm here as Croft's caretaker,' and was about to add 'and nothing else' when Diane sent her an understanding smile, and cut in on her half-finished statement:

'I'm sure you take good care of him too. You're different. I can't see any of the women he used to go around with getting their talons messed up with flour, if that was an apple pie you were making for him when I called.'

Mercy fretted for some time after Diane had gone. She hadn't stayed long after her remark about the apple pie, but had returned, though, to the question of where it was they had met. It was a very relieved Mercy who closed the door on her when she left. It had taken all her wits to keep her from knowing, to keep those grey eyes from clouding over again should she mention Hilary's name, and this had left no room for her to make it clear that she truly was there solely as a caretaker.

Croft had desired her, she knew that, Mercy thought, not letting in the voice of conscience that would have prodded, had she let it, that the wanting had been mutual. But what if he heard from Diane that she had allowed her to think what she had? What would he think? Would he think she had been having second thoughts about the way she had screamed at him to get out of her bedroom the other morning? He hadn't answered her when she'd asked for the duplicate key to her bedroom, had he? Did he still desire her? Was he perhaps thinking it was only a matter of time?

Aware that the more she thought about it, the more wild her imagination was going to go, Mercy ate her meal still brooding over what Diane might say to Croft.

But it was when she got around to thinking what Croft might say to Diane, that the urge she had been restraining to ring him to tell him that Diane had left with a totally erroneous impression, finally became irresistible.

She had to ring him, tip him off. Not that he was likely to slip up and tell his sister where they had met. But—he had no way of knowing, unless she rang him, what she had told Diane of their meeting.

Wondering if she would hear a different female answer the phone this time, though of course he could have smoothed things over with Felicia Woodward, Mercy dialled his number.

To hear him answer the phone in person left her uncertain what to say for a second or two, then, 'Hello, Croft. It's me, Mercy,' she said, and thought she heard a swift intake of breath as though he had just banged his hand on something. Then one short sharp word was being clipped down the line:

'Trouble?'

Did he think it was only when she was in trouble that she contacted him? Her brow wrinkled as the thought came, why else should she ring him? 'No, well, not really,' she denied, hating to admit she was in anyway bothered by anything. Then she heard amusement in his voice, as making no attempt to hurry her, he observed:

'I hardly think you've brought yourself to phone me just for a social chat.'

'I'm your employee, remember,' she found herself snapping, since she didn't want this conversation to take that route at all.

'You've found a mouse in the kitchen,' he said, not taking her seriously in the slightest.

'I have not,' she said tartly. 'Neither is the guttering blocked up, nor has a window broken.'

'So you *have* rung up for a chat.'

She wanted to brain him; what she had to say was serious. But she hadn't wanted to say it bluntly, would far rather have preferred to lead up to it.

'I've got better things to do than that,' she said acidly. And found herself blurting out then, and with some heat, 'Your sister visited me this afternoon. She thinks I'm living here as your mistress.'

That should put paid to his cheerful humour, she thought, unrepentant in the pause that followed her unwrapped statement. But she was to feel quite violent towards him, when, good humour still in his voice, she heard him say:

'Diane always did say I had excellent taste.'

'That wasn't what she intimated this afternoon,' she snapped back sourly.

'Which must mean, since you have obviously been talking me over, that she thinks you're a decided improvement.'

'We didn't have y . . .' She checked. 'You barely came into the conversation,' she said loftily. Then, thinking that with him in a baiting mood, they would never get anywhere, she swallowed down the ire he had aroused in her, and went on more evenly. 'Look, Croft, the only reason I called you is because I thought you should know what Diane thinks—about me living here.'

'So now you've told me.' She refused to slam the phone down as every instinct demanded. Then heard him add, a query there, 'But I can't quite understand how you let her go away with that impression.'

It sounded very much to her as if she was being taken to task for having done such a thing. It occurred to her that while he wouldn't mind everyone knowing he was Felicia Woodward's lover, he would be saying 'Do me a favour' if anyone suggested that the unsophisticated Mercy Yeomans was his bed-mate.

'I couldn't help it,' she said, hating herself for suddenly sounding defensive.

'You didn't want Diane to think what she did, did you?' he asked quietly.

'What do you take me for?' she flashed, letting him know she would be saying 'Do me a favour' too. 'Of course I didn't.'

'Then why, for heaven's sake,' he barked, suddenly sounding tough, 'let . . .'

'I—for most of the time she was here, I was afraid of upsetting her,' she butted in. Not waiting for another tough-sounding remark, she rushed on, 'What with that, and her thinking what she did, it carried little weight when I did get round to telling her I was your caretaker.' Her voice was subdued when she tacked on, 'She thought I meant something else.'

Croft had been digesting what she said as she spoke, Mercy saw, and his voice was sharp when ignoring that 'something else' Diane had read into her presence at the cottage, he asked:

'You were afraid of upsetting her—why?'

'Why, because of what you told me, of course,' Mercy snapped, no longer on the defensive.

'About . . .?'

'About Diane and her husband.'

'You spoke of what I told you—to her!' he asked, sounding incredulous.

'Thanks for your mighty opinion of me,' she retorted hotly. 'Of course I didn't mention it. That's how I didn't get round to telling her at the start that I am your employee.'

'You've lost me somewhere,' he said, and abruptly instructed, 'Start at the beginning.'

She took a deep breath. If one of them didn't hang on to their temper, then blue sparks would be striking off the phone.

'Diane asked had I known you long,' she said coldly. 'I started to say we had met at Hilary's wedding. Then I realised just in time that I might be opening up wounds that hadn't healed over yet.'

'Ah,' said Croft, good humour back there in his voice, as neatly he tied up everything she had told him and came up with the right answer. 'I see,' he said. Then a warmer note came into his voice, 'What a sweet darling you are, Mercy Yeomans.'

'I am, aren't I,' she said, and proved it—by slamming down the phone on him.

The feeling of moodiness, rare in her, that had gone to bed with Mercy, awakened with her the following morning. Only minutes after she had slammed down the phone on Croft last night, she had got round to seeing his 'What a sweet darling you are' as not being warm as it had hit her ears at the time, but as being sarcastic.

Who does he think he is, she thought, not for the first time as, her breakfast things washed, the kitchen tidy, she decided to take herself off for a walk.

And what sort of opinion did he have of her anyway? He'd been ready to believe—before she'd put him right—that she had repeated to Diane everything he had told her about her troubled marriage. Been ready to believe she had purposely let Diane believe what she had about them.

He could go to hell, she thought in hot mutiny, as she climbed over a stile. It didn't say much for the type of woman he was used to consorting with if that was his opinion of the female sex, that they didn't have one scrap of sensitivity one to another.

That thought naturally brought her mind on to Felicia Woodward. Hard-faced bitch, she thought, slightly amazed that she should think that of a woman she barely knew. Though having gone one round with her, she didn't imagine that Felicia would have put Diane's sensitivities before her own—if Felicia had any.

She was glad, without knowing why, that Felicia and Croft had split. Though she changed her opinion rapidly about that when she discovered the thought going through her head that Felicia wasn't good enough for him. Of course she was good enough for him, what was she thinking about, they were a pair well matched—they deserved each other.

Her walk hadn't done her the least bit of good, she decided when she arrived back at Lupin Cottage. Her spirits were still at a low ebb. Surely it had nothing at all to do with the thought that had come to her on her way home, the thought that maybe Felicia and Croft had made it up.

There's too much traffic around here, she thought, when midway through the afternoon she heard the sound of a car pulling up outside. And she had told Croft she loved the solitude!

Knowing it wouldn't be him—she'd like to bet she was the first person ever to have put the phone down on him—Mercy did not stir until she heard a knock on the front door. She wasn't in the mood for company, and if it was Felicia Woodward come for round two, she was in just the right fettle for her. Though it might be Diane, so she had better try to cheer up; that poor girl didn't look too much as though life was a barrel of laughs.

Ready to force a smile, though not seriously thinking it would be Diane, Mercy opened the door. And got the shock of her life to see Philip Bailey standing there.

'Philip!' she exclaimed, going slightly pink at the remembrance of their last meeting.

'Hope you don't mind, Mercy, but Miss Sefton gave me your address. A letter came for you from your parents, and I told Miss Sefton I'd bring it over for you.'

'Oh, Philip, you needn't have bothered,' she said softly, touched by his kindness, her eyes on his thin familiar face. 'It would have been all right to re-direct it.'

He cleared his throat. 'That wasn't the only reason I came.'

'Oh,' she said. And, feeling at a loss as she took the blue air-mail envelope from him, 'You'd better come in.'

Never in her life having felt uncomfortable with him, she invited him to take a seat, and found she was searching for something to say as she sat down and waited for him to tell her why he had taken the two-hour drive to see her.

'Your mother's foot,' she said, after a struggle remembering his mother's accident, 'is it any better?'

'Oh yes, yes, much, much,' said Philip, causing her only then to recall how often in the past Philip had repeated himself. 'Luckily it wasn't such a serious sprain as we had first thought. She's up and about again now.'

Another stilted silence threatened. 'That's good,' she said, when he did nothing to fill the gap.

'Yes indeed, yes indeed.'

'You—er—wanted to see me about something?' she prompted.

'The money.'

'The money,' she repeated, and thought, he's got me at it now. Then she was remembering how dear Philip had been to her, was still, she reminded herself, and she put aside the whimsical thought that they sounded like a record with the needle stuck. 'What money, Philip?' she asked seriously.

'Our savings. I've drawn it all out. I've brought you your half.'

'Oh,' she said, surprised. Though, on consideration, she was not really surprised. She had never doubted Philip's honesty.

With her permission he pulled up a low table, and though she protested that he shouldn't, he began to count the money out. And when that was done, he proceeded to go into minute detail of how the interest had accrued. He baffled her with his talk of percentages, so that in the end her eyes glazed over, and she emitted an occasional, 'Yes, I see,' so that he would think she was still with him.

Had he always been like this, she wondered? So pedantic? So—so boring? It shocked her that she could think him boring, so that when his itemising of accounts was over, she sent him a beaming smile as an apology for her unspoken thoughts. And that seemed to be the cue he had been waiting for.

'I didn't really come about the money,' he said, jerkily grabbing one of her hands. Mercy left her hand in his clammy grip. There was nothing to be afraid of with Philip, she knew that.

'Why then, Philip?' she gently asked. 'Why did you come?'

'I'm—lonely without you,' he confessed, his hand squeezing hers.

'Oh, Philip,' she said softly, feeling the prick of tears behind her eyes, realising that she had been right in telling herself that she didn't want to marry him. She hadn't felt any loneliness at his being no longer around.

'Come back to Ravensmere with me, Mercy,' he said, giving her hand another convulsive squeeze.

'I can't,' she said simply, and knew it for the truth.

'Yes, yes, you can,' said Philip, who as far as she could remember had never contradicted anyone, 'Yes, you can.'

But Mercy shook her head. Aside from the fact she had nowhere in Ravensmere to live, what was there to go back for? 'No,' she said. But before she could say that she wouldn't go back because she just didn't want to, he was again contradicting her.

'Yes, Mercy, yes,' he said. 'And if you're worried because you'll have nowhere to live, you can come and live with Mother and me.' She shuddered at the prospect, but, not noticing, he went on to astonish her. 'I know we haven't enough money yet to set up a home of our own. But we can get married and live with Mother until we have. And with your salary and mine from the school . . .'

'Philip.' She hadn't the heart to tell him she had resigned, but she had to stop him. 'What are you saying?' she asked, sure he couldn't really understand himself what he was trying to convey.

'I'm saying that I'm prepared to forgive you,' he said,

his words sounding pompous in her ears as again he
squeezed her hand.

'F-forgive,' she stammered.

'For what you've done,' he said.

'For . . .'

'Mother said I would be a fool to take you back,' he
went on to inform her, while she was staggering at the
pomposity in him which she never had before seen.

'You—don't think you should take your mother's
advice?' she asked weakly, a nightmare picture of living
in the same house with an unforgiving Mrs Bailey
enough to put her, or any girl, off.

'You're sorry for what you did,' he said, 'I know you
are. It will . . .'

Why she broke in to cut him off before he could say
more, she wasn't certain—some sort of inverted pride,
she thought. But cut him off she did, and she felt as
incredulous as he looked when the bald words tripped
off her tongue.

'I'm not sorry for what I did, Philip,' she said, 'Not
at all sorry.'

'What!'

He looked stupefied, she saw, as if it was the last
thing he had expected to hear. She was feeling a little
that way herself for saying what she had, when what
she should be telling him was that she and Croft had
never . . .

She then saw that she had no need to tell Philip
anything. For his face showed quite clearly, when his
shock receded, that he had received her message that
she didn't want to marry him, that he had made a
fruitless journey.

All at once, he wasn't the Philip Bailey she knew at
all. For he was on his feet and was dragging her to her
feet. Had his arms around her, and was saying as his
head came nearer:

'You think I can't be passionate like that chap you

gave yourself to, don't you? Just because I've respected both of us too much to do anything we shouldn't, you think I don't have passion in me, don't you?'

'It isn't that . . .'

But his mouth on hers stopped her from saying anything else. And he was kissing her in a way he had never kissed her before—and Mercy felt saddened by it.

She tried to push him away, knowing that, honest though Philip was, he wasn't being honest now. His passion was assumed, put on as though in view of her turning him down he thought that to be passionate would be the way to make her change her mind. But he wasn't a passionate man, she realised then, there simply wasn't a natural passion in him. He was forcing himself to be like this, because he thought it was what she wanted.

To struggle was useless, she discovered. One gentle kiss from Croft had the power to stir her more than the onslaught Philip was making on her mouth. She made herself stand still, was unprotesting, the thought coming that that was the quickest way to get through to him.

She felt sadder than ever that it had come to this. She would have liked to spare Philip, who valued self-respect above everything, the disgust he would have with himself when any minute now he would see he was wasting his time.

Suddenly, she was aware that his hands had started to move on her. And all sadness in her vanished, anger only was there that he wasn't stopping, that he could think that this was what she wanted from him.

But it was in that moment of his trembling hands nearing her breasts, before she could knock them away, that both of them heard a sound that told them someone had come silently into the room. And that someone was watching them.

'If you have to act like a dog with a bitch in heat,' thundered a furious voice that made Philip let go of her, that made them both spin round, 'would you mind doing it off my property?'

Shaken rigid to see Croft Latimer standing there obviously having let himself in with his own key, for several seconds neither of them had anything to say.

Then as colour seared Mercy's face at what Croft thought he had seen, shame covering her at the implication of his comment, her anger against Philip was matched by an equal anger against Croft. And Mercy stared at Croft for only a moment longer, then— uproar broke out.

CHAPTER EIGHT

THREE angry people all blasting away at the same time left little room for any but the basic points to get through.

'You!' exclaimed Philip.

And having recognised Croft as the man he had seen in bed with Mercy, he turned from Croft to vent his spleen on her. Mercy wasted no time in attacking Croft for daring to describe her as a bitch on heat. While Croft, not waiting for his turn, bellowed the accusation at her that she was running the place as a love-nest behind his back. Philip went on to revile her with the accusation:

'You're having an affair with him, aren't you? You're *living* with him!'

Mercy, taken dumb for a moment, saw Croft's sharp glance go from her to Philip, and back again. She saw some of the thunder leave his expression, and knew that his brain cogs were as active as ever, as Philip continued:

'It wasn't an isolated incident I walked in on at your flat. You have never stopped what began there, have . . .'

Having seen a side of Philip that day she didn't like, Mercy wasn't any nearer to finding her voice as she discovered that he could be as nasty as the next when upset. But too shaken for the moment to defend herself, she heard Croft come in to chop him off; what he said doing nothing to make her any more pleased with the pair of them.

'I haven't done anything to the lady you wouldn't have done if I hadn't come in and caught you at it,' he told him, anger still in him, but with an ice there which to Mercy's ears sounded threatening.

But as it dawned on her that he was as good as telling Philip that they had laid together as lovers, her fury broke.

That she had only minutes earlier let Philip think the self-same thing, had nothing to do with it. Suddenly she was fed up with both of them. Fed up and furious.

Her fury was evident in the way she stormed past them, taking no heed that two sets of eyes had followed and watched in astonishment as she threw the door wide. And—regardless that Croft had more right to be there than she had—she turned, her eyes spitting fire.

'Out!' she ordered. And while Philip made a small movement, and Croft stood firm, her voice rose as she demanded, 'Both of you—*out*!'

Had they waited a second longer to shift themselves, she knew she would have marched out herself and would never have come back. But she did not have to take such action. For suddenly Croft had caught hold of Philip's lapel with his right hand, not sending her mercury any lower when she thought she saw his lips quirk the moment before he docilely said:

'It rather looks as though we have been given the order of the boot.'

'Solitude!' Mercy muttered angrily, slamming the front door behind Croft after he had pushed Philip out in front of him. 'It's like Piccadilly Circus round here!'

Neither knowing or caring where either of them went, she pushed the catch up on the door, so that no one could get back in with or without a key. Then she stood there for some minutes fuming against men in general, and two in particular.

Then, feeling weepy all of a sudden, feeling cheapened, she took herself off upstairs with no concrete aim in view. Ten minutes later she came down again. Her temper had cooled, but she still wasn't very sure that she wasn't going to cry.

She relatched the stairs door behind her, wondering, had she really ordered Croft out of his own home? Then a sound from the kitchen had her darting there to see that Croft had come in by the back door; no sign of Philip.

Temper ready to rear again, she opened her mouth, then closed it. She did not want to laugh, but having seen war in her eyes, at just that moment Croft pulled the dish mop from behind his back. Tied to it was a white handkerchief.

'Clown,' she muttered. But her lips having parted, she could do nothing about the way they tweaked upwards.

Then just as suddenly, tears were pricking her eyes. 'Oh, Croft,' she said, for no reason, and was trying desperately hard to get herself under control.

A teardrop strayed to her cheek as she turned away, ready to bolt for her bedroom. But she didn't get as far as the kitchen door. Strong arms came about her, turned her before she could make it.

'I . . .' she said, and was hushed quiet.

'Not happy with scenes, are you?' he said softly, and gently cradled her head to his chest.

'Is anybody?' she mumbled, but made no attempt to pull out of his arms.

His arms seemed oddly comforting somehow, she thought, which added to her laughing, crying confusion, when she recalled how she had hated being in Philip's arms so recently, and that she had been as mad at Croft as she had been at Philip.

But she no longer felt angry, more—mixed up. She knew she should be telling Croft she was all right now, knew she should pull out of his arms. But she didn't want to, did not yet feel 'all right'. Was not sure, though she had managed to hold her tears in check, that she wasn't in for a good howl—and she hardly knew why.

With Croft gently holding her, nothing in any way

sexual, she thought, in the way he occasionally smoothed her hair, she tried to get herself together.

'I'm fine now,' she said, when minutes had ticked by and he had made no move to release her.

A gentle hand came beneath her chin, tilting her head so that he could see into her face. 'You don't look it,' he said softly. 'Those big brown eyes tell me you're still wondering how in Hades all that happened.' He smiled, not an atom of mockery about him. 'Care to stay where you are and tell me how it all came about? How Bailey came to know where to find you?'

Mercy dropped her eyes, and very soon had her head back in its comfortable position in his chest. It wasn't a thing she wanted to talk about, but after a moment of not saying anything, the very fact that Croft was letting her lean on him for a while until the confusion in her righted itself; the very fact he wasn't prodding, or prying, or trying to coax it out of her; the way he was silently saying she could use him to let it all out if she cared to; slowly at first, she began to tell him what had happened since she had opened the front door to Philip.

'He said he had brought me a letter from my parents,' she said, and explained how she had gone back to Ravensmere to vacate her flat, and had left her forwarding address with Miss Sefton. 'Then—then he said he had come to bring me my share of our joint savings.'

'That was the money I saw on the table in the other room.'

She nodded. 'Then Philip said the letter and the money weren't why he had come at all . . .' Her voice faded as she recalled the way Philip had kissed her.

She felt the arms about her tighten briefly, and the next moment Croft was saying, not needing an answer, 'He came to ask you to marry him.'

'He said—he would forgive me,' she remembered. And there was silence again for some moments. Then

Croft pounced on the point that she had known all along his intelligence had picked up:

'But you didn't tell him there was nothing to forgive, did you, Mercy?'

She evaded the answer; he knew it anyway. She felt less comfortable in his arms then. 'Philip thought . . .' she began, and had to go on, though she was backing out of Croft's arms, as she finished, 'He thought it was passion I wanted.'

'And that's where I came in,' he said, letting her go, letting his arms fall from her.

'Bitch in heat,' she reminded him. But she no longer felt angry with him for his remark.

'Do all the men in your life beg for forgiveness?' he asked, his mouth starting to twitch, so she knew he was joking about being 'a man in her life', and Philip had been forgiving her, not the other way around. Then Croft's eyes were going over her face that had been pale up in her bedroom, 'You still don't look on an even keel yet,' he observed. 'Why not go and read your letter while I make you a cup of tea?'

'You certainly know how to treat a girl,' she quipped, trying to pretend that she could take a three-cornered row in her stride any day of the week.

'And you must be feeling better than you look,' he returned lightly. 'You're getting saucy again,' a reminder that she had ordered him out.

It was nice being fussed over, she thought, as taking an easy chair in the sitting room, she slit the envelope of her letter to the accompanying rattle of the tea-cups in the kitchen.

When he came in, pushing aside the money on the table so that he could set down the tray, she was surfacing from the effects of all that had gone on. Her mother's letter, so sane, so normal, the memory of her mother who had never raised her voice, her letter sounding just as she always sounded, had gone a good way to help. Perhaps she would go and pay them a visit, she thought, she had money enough to do that now. But, much as she would like to see her parents, she wasn't in any hurry to make a decision. She had plenty of time at her disposal, no need to rush at anything.

'I was tempted to lace it with sugar,' said Croft, handing her a cup of tea before sitting down with his own, 'but I thought you might not drink it if I did.'

'You think I'm in shock!'

'Let's say I think you feel a little degraded by that scene I was party to. That in my view you're still wondering how such a thing ever happened in your quiet, never-hurt-a-fly life.'

He had pegged it exactly. He knew, with a perception she hadn't credited him with, that that was precisely how she was feeling, and she realised that there must be very little about women that he hadn't learned. And from that 'never hurt a fly' comment, she guessed he must have thought her a softie when she had been careful not to say a word that would have his sister feeling a renewal of pain.

'Well—I'm fine again now,' she said, and took a sip of her tea, very nearly choking on it when he came back with:

'But if I leave you're going to spend the rest of the night going all over it again, aren't you?'

Just in case he had anything more shattering to say, hastily Mercy put down her cup. By the sound of it, he was debating whether or not to return to London that night.

'No, I won't,' she lied. 'I—er——' Her powers of invention dried up. 'I'm fine now,' was all she had left to reiterate.

'You don't look it,' he said bluntly. 'You're too pale. Upset still, I can see that.' Then he was asking, causing her heart to hammer, causing an unaccountable breathlessness in her, 'Would you like me to stay?'

Her answer should be no, she knew that. But Croft Latimer had the uncanny knack of making her tongue say the opposite of what she intended. Definitely she didn't want him to stay if his idea of staying meant what she thought he might be meaning.

Nowhere near to giving him his answer, watchful of her unwary tongue, she was saved making an instant decision, when Croft followed on:

'I don't particularly want to drive back to London tonight. Though I must get back before noon tomorrow.'

Felicia Woodward, she thought, he's got a date with her tomorrow. An unexpected, swift, piercing dart of jealousy hit her at the thought, and though not recognising it for the emotion it was until a minute later, she opened her mouth to tell him in no uncertain terms that if he was staying, then he was not sharing her bed. She discovered, when she did speak, that she was putting him right on that score in an entirely different fashion.

'I'll make sure to put my alarm clock in your room,' she said. But she saw, as he got her message, that far from being angry that any ideas he had had been scuppered, he was highly amused at the charming way she had acquainted him with the news.

His mouth started to curve, his eyes twinkled with humour. And suddenly she was on the receiving end of the most wonderful grin he had ever bestowed on her.

It was in that moment of knowing that Croft was not the sort to sulk because his plans had been thwarted, in that moment of receiving a warm smiling look, just for her, that she very nearly did go into shock. For it was then that the warning signs she had been heedless of came together to tell her what she had not seen. She was in love with Croft Latimer!

Instinctively her head went down as she covered that shattering moment of discovery by reaching for her teacup. Silently she prayed that if Croft noticed her hand had begun to shake, he would put it down to the shock he thought she had been under before. The last thing she wanted him to know was that that scene paled into insignificance compared to this!

Somehow or other she got through the next three or four minutes. Then, her cup empty, she scooped up the money Philip had left on the table, and muttering something about taking it upstairs, she went quickly, not giving a thought to the fact that she had left Croft with the washing up.

Up in her room she collapsed into a chair, the truth she couldn't ignore not going away, much as she willed it. She was in love with him! When it had begun to happen she had no idea. What it was about him that made her feel that way, she had no idea. He wasn't always kind, wasn't always pleasant the way, up until today, Philip had been. He had misled her dreadfully about that night they had slept in the same bed—but—she was in love with him, and would be, no matter what he did. It was just there, her love for him, and she had agreed to his spending the night in the cottage!

Whatever happened he must not discover how she felt about him, Mercy thought, ready to colour up on merely thinking of the embarrassment that would be hers if he did. It was certain he didn't feel that way about her. Why, he couldn't wait to be away tomorrow, if not because he had a date with Felicia Woodward, then she was confident it would be with some other female. Probably a lunch date, she thought, since he'd stated he had to be in London before noon.

She spent a further five minutes being torn apart by a jealousy which she admitted she had no right to. Then she realised that if she didn't put in an appearance downstairs soon, Croft might begin to wonder what was keeping her so long. She had to guard against his starting to wonder anything about her.

She would be pleasant, friendly, she thought, hoping as she left her room that he wouldn't say anything that would trigger the blushes that came too readily in his company. She didn't want him, with his clever brain, suspecting anything.

Pleasant and friendly, she thought, opening the stairs door, she didn't want to do anything to trigger off his ample aggression either. His aggression that might fire hers, and have her tongue going down unwary channels.

'Floor-boards safely back?' he questioned, rising from his chair when, the stairs door closed, she had turned into the room. His question had her foxed, and her puzzlement showed. 'I thought you'd been hiding the loot under the floor-boards,' he helped her out.

'Have I been that long?' she said guilelessly, offering no excuse purely because just seeing him confirmed what she already knew was in her heart, and caused her inventive powers to seize up, though at his prompting she had recalled that she had used taking the money up to her room as an excuse for going upstairs. 'I'll go and see what we can have for dinner,' she said, offering him a smile, needing a few more minutes alone to take hold of her self-control.

'I did think we'd have dinner out,' he said, which halted her and set her heart racing at the mere thought of being squired into town by him. Then with that charm of his, that little boy in him that knotted her insides, his mouth was curving into that crooked grin she loved, and he was saying, 'Though if you're offering to slave over a hot stove for me, I know which I'd prefer.'

He was leaving the choice to her, she could see that. Logic told her they'd better go out to eat. It was on the tip of her tongue to say she hadn't been out in an age.

'How are you with washing up?' she enquired. Logic was a puny ally when up against her emotions.

And she had to burst out laughing when he replied comically, looking pleased they were dining at home, 'I'm an expert,' because the tea-tray had been removed from the table, and she knew the cups wouldn't be waiting for her attention in the kitchen.

As it turned out, she wasn't left to do very much slaving over a hot stove. For Croft was a willing assistant, if a not very able one. He insisted on peeling the potatoes, muttering when he tried his skill with a potato peeler that it must be an art, opting instead to use a sharp knife, the thickness of the peel sending shudders through Mercy, though since he seemed to be enjoying the chore, she let him get on with it.

Hiding what was in her heart was easier than she had first thought. She was careful not to laugh too often at Croft's wit. He seemed in a light-hearted mood, but she didn't want him thinking her a grinning idiot when every comment he made brought laughter in her near the surface.

They ate in the kitchen, simply because that was where the only regular-sized table was. 'I should have brought some wine with me,' he remarked as he helped himself to the pepper and salt.

She almost said, 'Have you brought your razor?' but bit it back in time. This occasion was different for her, special, she didn't want to rake over ashes of what had gone before. It was this evening, this evening she wanted to remember.

'You didn't know you were going to stay?' she said instead. And receiving no reply, which she thought she hardly could since he had just put a piece of steak into his mouth, she went on to ask a question that had been in her mind for some time now. 'Why did you come, by the way?'

She felt herself colour, and found her plate of much interest when he didn't immediately answer. It was his property, for goodness' sake. He had every right to call when he wished, without having his caretaker question him. But ridiculous hope soared skywards as her eyes flew to him when at last he did reply.

'How could I keep away?' he asked, his eyes searching her carefully veiled ones before he lightly tacked on, 'When a little bird told me you had spent some time yesterday in preparing an apple pie, especially for me.'

Hope split asunder. 'I didn't . . .' she began automatically to protest. Then she saw he was teasing, that he had known the apple pie hadn't been made with him in mind. But his 'a little bird told me' showed her he had had knowledge of its existence before he had seen her put it in the oven to warm up.

'You've been in touch with Diane?'

'I thought I had better correct any wrong impressions she might have.'

'I—see,' said Mercy slowly. But she was hurt, and it showed.

She looked away, near to tears again, and wasn't sure she would be able to sit it out to the end of their meal. Then that hurt in her formed itself into anger, anger with herself, with him.

'Well, so long as Diane knows you don't take every little scrubber to bed, I'm sure you both feel very much better about it,' she snapped, flicking him a fiery glance, careless that instant aggression had reared in him too.

'What ever do you mean by that?' he questioned curtly.

'Exactly what I say,' she retaliated, her thoughts of being pleasant and friendly gone up in smoke. 'It didn't matter a damn to you if Philip, people who knew me, thought we'd been lovers. But you wouldn't want your sister, *your* friends, believing you had taken some village nonentity—your caretaker—to bed, would you?'

For a moment there, it looked as though Croft would leap out of his chair and slap her. His chair actually did grate back on the quarry stone floor. And then, though his jaw was thrust forward as he controlled the obvious urge and remained where he was, he took a long indrawn breath and icily told her:

'That your opinion of me is basement level I'll accept as my due for keeping quiet at a time when, had I spoken up, I could have saved you from mental anguish.' Very little left on his plate, he pushed it away, his action telling there that not only did he want nothing from her, but soon he would be returning to London. 'But,' he went on, his voice icier than ever, 'for the record, I'll tell you exactly why I did ring Diane. I rang her to put her straight about your position here. Not, as you so charmingly put it, because I didn't want her to think I was taking some 'little scrubber' to bed, but because in my respect for you, I had realised it was upsetting you that she should think you were my mistress.'

'You . . .' she managed to get out chokily, but that was all. She had been severely dressed down, and never had she felt so miserable. Love, of course, was the reason for her being so overly sensitive. Love had had her imagining slights which just weren't there.

'And,' Croft said, before she could get her apology out, 'you might as well know, while we're on the subject, that should Diane drop in to see you again, you will have no need to pussyfoot around. I have told her where we met, that you were bridesmaid at that wedding.'

He stood up then. It was at an end. And, bleeding inside, Mercy didn't want him to go, not like this. She opened her mouth to say she was sorry, and knew that wouldn't do any good either as he went to the sink top to collect his watch.

'W-would it do any good if—if I told you I respect you as well?' she heard herself ask. She saw he had halted, was still, his back to her, but knew that stillness didn't mean he wasn't going to leave.

Feeling utterly downcast, she tore her eyes from his back to stare unseeing down at the table. She heard him move, and knew there was nothing more to be said. Knew that what had started out as a light-hearted meal before she had spoiled it, had turned into something dreadful, and by her words, she was the cause of it.

Aware he had come to stand near, unconsciously she sighed. And when he stood, not moving away, unable to look up at him, she struggled hard, and found the words, 'Do—all the women in your life have to beg—for forgiveness?'

She guessed she had hoped to appeal to his sense of humour, even though he had looked too angry ever to be amused again by anything she said.

But unbelievably, though his voice was stiff, that icy note had gone when he questioned, 'You're apologising for daring to think what you did?'

'I'd wear sackcloth and ashes if I thought it would help.' She looked up at him then, her eyes moist with tears she was trying to hold back.

Surprise took her to see the coldness had gone from those grey eyes. A sort of panic gripped her, causing her eyes to widen, when suddenly the tension went from him, and he said softly:

'Don't look at me like that, Mercy Yeomans.' And when she offered a tentative smile, having no idea how she was looking but too overjoyed that he wasn't still mad at her to do anything about it, he said, 'I'm sorely tempted to kiss you, only I'm afraid you would misunderstand it.'

Abruptly she lowered her eyes lest he should see she wanted him to kiss her. She didn't think she would misunderstand it, but she could not risk it.

'I wouldn't want any more misunderstandings,' she said, her voice rather wobbly. And when he hadn't moved, afraid she might soon be pleading with him to kiss her, she said, 'You haven't tasted my apple pie yet.'

That he was staying the night after all didn't need to be said. It was there in his action when it was he who went over to the oven and brought the pie to the table

They had coffee in the sitting room. Croft, dismissing the brief storm that had blown up, soon had her forgetting about it too. Though once more she was aware that she had to be on her guard in case he discovered how it was with her.

They were on their second cup of coffee when, having been drawn out by him to reveal the idea that had flitted through her mind of visiting her parents, she heard him say:

'You wouldn't go and leave me without a caretaker would you?'

He sounded serious, although she knew he was teasing. They both knew hers wasn't a permanent job, but, afraid he would see how much she wanted him to be serious, how desperately she wanted him to ask her to stay, she answered lightly, 'It was only an idea,' then quickly turned the conversation away from herself. 'I expect you travel widely in your job?'

'Funny you should say that,' he said, and then revealed the reason he had to be in London before noon the next day. 'I'm off to the States tomorrow for three weeks.'

'You're . . .' She held down her surprise, delighted that he didn't have a date with some sophisticated female, but despair coming to mingle with her delight because she wouldn't have the chance of seeing him for three weeks. Had he been staying in London he might have popped down . . . Thoughts of the glamorous females he might meet in America came to stamp on other thoughts and had her fighting to survive. 'It will be a working three weeks?' she queried as brightly as she could.

'Not all of it, I hope,' he said, which was no help in sending that little green demon on its way. 'Though I do have a fairly tight schedule.'

After his bombshell about leaving the country
morrow, he went on to charm, to enchant her, talking
ghtly, easily about his various trips abroad. But it was
hen she caught herself sending him a softly laughing
ok after some witticism he had made, that Mercy
ought she had better go to bed.

It wasn't what she wanted to do—three weeks seemed
ght-years away—she wanted to snatch every moment
e could with him. But her guard was sinking lower
d lower.

'We country girls go to bed early,' she said into the
mpanionable silence that had fallen, accompanying
r words by getting up from her chair.

Croft's face didn't show the disappointment her crazy
art was hoping for. Though his compliment went
ite a way to make up for it, as he too rose.

'In your case it's not because you need your beauty
ep,' he replied.

Then her mouth dried, her heart beat frantically,
hen he came over and took her hand in his. For it was
ter he had raised her hand to his lips and kissed it,
at their eyes came into direct contact. And there was
ch a burning look in his eyes, a flame there, that she
uldn't fail to know that he wanted her.

For many seconds she was incapable of moving, of
eaking even. There was an electricity charging the air
they wordlessly looked at each other, an electricity
e could feel, almost touch. Half a step forward and
e would be sunk, she knew it. Just as she knew with
verwhelming certainty in that moment that Croft felt
at same electricity in the air, and that he would not
ject her.

She was still dithering on the edge of taking that tiny
ep forward, when he let go her hand, and taking a
ep back he did exactly that—he rejected her.

'Go to bed, Mercy,' he said, the lightness that had
en part of him ever since their row in the kitchen,

now sounding strained as tightly he added, 'It's been an emotional day for you.'

She opened her mouth. She had been meaning sluice her face in the kitchen, but that no longer seem important, 'G-good-night,' she said, and fled.

CHAPTER NINE

WHEN Mercy awoke the next morning, her first thought was to wonder if Croft had come up to bed last night. She hadn't heard him on the stairs, and she had been awake for hours.

She got out of bed and tied her robe around her, those thoughts that had spun in her head before sleep had claimed her, reforming in her mind. Croft had seen when she had stood frozen, unable to move after he had kissed her hand, that her emotions were going out of control. That he thought it was because of that scene with him and Philip, that scene in the kitchen, was a bonus to her pride. But the trouble was, she could only love him more, because when desiring her as she had to know he had, he had also seen she wouldn't have been liking him very much this morning if he had taken advantage of what he termed had been 'an emotional day for her'.

Though whether she would not have liked him very much this morning had he followed up what had been burning in his eyes, was a moot point, she thought. She was anxious that he should not leave before she had the chance to so much as see him. She put all thoughts aside as she tightened the belt of her robe, and left her room.

Croft was already in the kitchen when Mercy went in, ready to make his breakfast. He had made his own breakfast, she saw, and had almost finished eating it.

'I was going to make that for you,' she said without thinking.

'And I was going to bring you a cup of tea in bed,' he said with equal honesty, 'only . . .' He left it there, his

eyes telling her nothing. But she knew he was
remembering the last time he had come into her
bedroom and awoken her.

'Only I tend to be a cross-patch first thing in the
morning,' she said lightly, her own eyes revealing
nothing as her heart-beats changed from double time to
triple as the thought hit—did he still desire her this
morning? Was that why . . .?

'Something like that,' he said, getting to his feet and
making for the door, muttering something about having
left his car keys on the dressing table upstairs.

That meant he would be off soon, she thought,
knowing she was going to have to hide the despondency
that thought brought. Automatically she began to clear
the table. Oh, how foolish her heart was! All Croft's
desiring her last night was nothing more than a
culmination of empathy that had built up between them
after their row, and that was all there was to it.

She had her hands in the washing-up bowl when she
heard the stairs door go, indicating he would join her at
any moment. She knew he had come to say goodbye,
heard him come into the kitchen. But, her heart aching,
she didn't want to say goodbye, with only the vaguest
idea of when she would see him again.

Then suddenly, aware as he must be that she knew he
was in the room, Croft had come over to her. She felt
his arms come around her waist, and knew control was
never more needed. She was having to resist with all her
might the impulse to lean back against him, the urge to
feel his chest at her head.

'Are you not going to turn round and wish me
Happy Landings, Mercy Yeomans?' he asked softly, the
words whispered close to her ear.

What could she do? She turned. Turned in the circle
of his arms, hiding what was in her heart as she looked
up at him. 'Happy Landings, Croft Latimer,' she said
obediently.

'Would you send me away without permitting me to do what last night I held myself back from doing?' he queried, his manner gently teasing.

Already on the way to being sunk, softly she said, 'What sort of a girl do you think I . . .' She felt his mouth on hers, not passionate, not cool. But warm, life-giving. It was a kiss she could only think of as beautiful.

But it was too soon over. Croft was putting her away from him, his eyes seeming to be photographing her face when for long seconds he looked at her. Then his hand came to touch the side of her face. 'Be good while I'm away,' he said. Then he was gone.

The week that followed Croft's departure for America was a week in which, for Mercy, his physical absence was filled by his being constantly there in her thoughts.

Would it always be like this, she wondered, recalling how Philip had once had to go away, and how though she had looked forward to his return, the waiting had never been like this.

Waiting? She was to query, when the second week got under way. What in creation did she think she was waiting for? Was she supposing for a minute that just because Croft had shown himself physically attracted to her, there was anything to wait for? Why, it was probably little more than propinquity that caused that male in him to stir itself, anyway. And he would have far better things to do when he returned than to pay a visit to the cottage.

Even while these thoughts were rambling around in her head, Mercy was pondering a counter argument. Lupin Cottage was *his* bolt hole. The place where he came when he needed to restock that vitality in him. The place he occasionally came when he wanted a break from the hectic business whirl. Surely, she argued, after three weeks on a business merry-go-round in the States—her mind refused to admit thoughts of the glamorous females he could well make time to take around—he would be ready for the relaxing solitude of Abbeybridge?

It was on the Friday of that second week, when Mercy got out of bed to go downstairs, Croft her constant companion still, that it came to her that she was being more than a little crass to be going on as she was. Any passing attraction he had felt for her had to be just that and no more. What was she hoping for? Did she think, for goodness' sake, having seen the type of woman he went for, the type of woman he had been going to ask to marry him, that she could in any way compete with the smarter than smart Felicia Woodwards of this world?

Needing to tire herself physically, Mercy took herself off for a long walk, the way she had many times since Croft had gone, her mind full of the hopelessness of even thinking of competing.

At two she returned to the cottage and knew a 'No contest' had been declared. Nature had favoured her with a figure she wasn't unhappy with, a clear complexion and a face she had no complaints about either. But she didn't have that air of uppity poise that must appeal to Croft, and if she tried from now until next year, she knew she would never have it. And she didn't know whether it was because she was just too sensitive to other people's feelings, or too proud, but whatever it was, she knew she wasn't going to try.

And that meant, she thought, staring glumly out of the window, that she had better put her thinking cap on—the other cap, the one that didn't have 'For exclusive thoughts of Croft' written on it—and get down to making plans for her future.

For a start, she thought, not minimising how she was going to feel at leaving Lupin Cottage, she had better do something about finding somewhere else to live. It couldn't make her feel any less wretched than she felt at the moment. But while she remained, she knew that once those three weeks were up, she would be straining her ears every minute of the day hoping to hear the sound of his car pulling up.

Wrapped in a world where her thoughts were tossed this way and that, the logical thought emerged, pride pressing her to act on it, that it would be far better for her to leave before Croft returned to England. She nearly shot out of her skin when the telephone, which hadn't rung once throughout her stay, suddenly shrilled into her tortuous thoughts.

It had to be Croft, was her first ridiculous thought, her heart pounding so loudly in her ears she doubted whether she would hear anything that was said. Common sense came to calm her. Any number of people could know the telephone number, she thought. Diane for one, Felicia Woodward for one unappealing other.

Her heart acted up again the moment she heard Croft's voice. But having been deep in depressing thoughts of vacating his property, those thoughts were still with her tempering the excitement in her on hearing him, so that she was able to say, and be proud of the even way she said it;

'You're not due back yet.'

'I got finished sooner than I expected.'

Just hearing his voice was making her weak. She grabbed for a chair and sat down. 'A successful trip, I hope?'

'Completely,' he replied, and little green darts pierced her as she took that to mean socially as well as businesswise.

'I'm—glad,' she said. And found that where before she had been able to chat away with him, suddenly there was a constriction in her throat, so that even if she could have thought of something light to say to him, she would not have been able to.

'What I'm ringing for,' he said, when a moment had passed and nothing else had come from her, 'is to ask you to get some groceries in for me.'

For two glorious seconds her heart did cartwheels. That must mean he was coming down. Then fear of giving herself away by word or deed came rushing in. Thoughts returned of how she had been going to leave. And a more terrible thought; could he, since he must know she could stretch her supplies to feed two, could he be bringing someone else with him? Oh dear, she thought, jealousy screaming through her, she just couldn't take staying in the tiny cottage to watch him giving Felicia Woodward that same burning, desiring look he had scorched her with.

'Mercy! Are you there?'

'I—just went to—get some paper for your grocery list,' she lied, then took down the things he required on the pad that was already there, while at the same time her mind was coping with the chant of 'I must get away, I must get away. I must . . .'.

'That the lot?' she enquired brightly, looking down the extensive list that told her without a doubt that he intended to feed someone in style.

'Have I forgotten anything, d'you think?' he enquired.

A spurt of anger, at him, at herself, at Felicia Woodward, she knew not who, had her struggling to hold back to suggest a couple of gallons of milk if it was that particular cat he was bringing with him.

'Your list seems fairly comprehensive,' she said evenly, adding, 'I'll see to it before I leave.'

'Leave!' Pure aggression came barking down the line. 'Where the hell do you think you're going?'

'You won't want me around if you're—you're bringing—company with you.'

'Com . . .' He broke off, and Mercy hung on. He didn't have to tell her who he was bringing with him.

She wasn't sure she wanted to know anyway. But the first real smile she had known for nearly two weeks was there on her mouth when she heard, aggression gone, his quietly spoken, 'I'm not bringing anyone with me, Mercy.' And while she was still bathing in the warmth that comment brought, 'I need you, Mercy. You wouldn't deprive me of my—caretaker—would you?'

'Wouldn't dream of it,' she said, quite happily.

But that was then. An hour later, stacking the last of the things she had purchased from the versatile village store, she had hit the ground with a bump. 'I need you, Mercy' had taken on a very different connotation from what she had blindly wanted him to mean. Since then she had inserted 'want' for the word 'need'.

Well, she wanted him too. Shortly after that thought, she was throwing a few things into a weekened case, and was driving away from Lupin Cottage.

The tears she spent that weekend, the yearning, the longing in her to be back at the cottage and not in the randomly chosen country hotel forty miles away to which she had fled, were to make that weekend the most miserable of her whole existence.

And yet nothing would have made her return until she knew Croft had gone back to London. Her love for him meant more than just the bodily satisfaction of her needs, his needs. Even while her love for him readily accepted that a place was there in that love to fulfil the passion he had that one time aroused in her, her love for him meant more than that to her.

Night-time was the worst, Mercy discovered. Night-time when the hotel was quiet, everyone seemingly settled but her. How easy, yet how difficult, it would have been to give in, to go to her car and keep her foot down on the accelerator until she got to Abbeybridge.

After a tormented Saturday night spent in snatching what sleep her Croft-filled mind would allow, daylight brought with it confirmation that she was right to have taken to her heels.

Croft would be leaving the cottage late that afternoon, she thought, fairly certain he would have stayed till then. His need for a rest from his labours must be all tied up with his reason for leaving London in the first place—that she wasn't there wouldn't have altered that, she thought.

But aware of her weakness where he was concerned, and just in case he had decided to leave his departure for London until early on Monday morning, she thought she had better stay where she was too.

Thinking Croft was now back in London, Mercy spent a better night on Sunday, and woke on Monday refreshed in body, though not any more rested in mind.

Having paid her hotel bill, she set her car in the direction of Abbeybridge, knowing she would wander all over the cottage picturing Croft in every room when she got there.

But in picturing him sitting in one of the easy chairs as he must have been at the weekend, picturing him making himself a cup of tea in the kitchen, there had not been one thought in her mind that he might still be there when she got back.

That was why, when she turned her car up the track to Lupin Cottage, she got the shock of her life to see his car was still there!

And having stopped her car, she was to spend several moments in agitated dithering. There wasn't any way she could turn her car round in the narrow track and go back the way she had come, she thought, too shattered by the sight of the Mercedes for it to enter her mind that she had a reverse gear. She was still nowhere near to being all of one piece when she saw Croft come striding from the cottage. Obviously he had seen her from a window, but by the fierce look of him, he had nothing but one hundred per cent aggression riding him.

Too paralysed to move, she was sitting dumbfounded when he wrenched open the car door. She was still trying to get over the shock that he wasn't miles away, when furious words came roaring in her ears.

'Where the hell have you been?'

His harsh words acted on her like a cup of sugar-filled tea, bringing her rapidly out of shock. She brought her chin up high as the first coherent thought activated in her head. She knew exactly why he was so all fired up—she had put paid to any ideas he'd had of a cosy little twosome weekend.

She left her car and pushed past him, her nose in the air, hurt that that was the extent of his regard for her. Then she felt his hand on her arm propelling her forward, as though he had thought better of berating her outside, but couldn't wait to get her inside to sort her out.

'Well?' he snarled, the front door barely closed behind them.

'Well what?' she challenged stiffly. She could see she had done nothing to relieve his fury, when, his eyes like shafts of steel, he roared, '*Where* have you been?'

'There's no need to shout,' she flared, her cool deserting her, sickness invading, the thought returning that the only reason he was upset was because she had denied him his plans for the weekend. 'It's no business of yours where I've been,' she yelled, not backing down when she saw he looked ready to strangle her for not giving him the answers he wanted. 'Even caretakers are allowed some time off,' she threw at him. And then had to swallow, for, his eyes glinting with a demoniacal fury, Croft took a few steps nearer.

But just when it looked as though he would cover the few yards that separated them, he halted, seeming to make a supreme effort not to come any closer for fear he might set about her.

'Damn you,' he gritted through clenched teeth, his

hands forming tight fists at his side, 'I'm not paying you to slink off on some illicit weekend with . . .'

'Illicit weekend!' she echoed, incredulity in her eyes at his nerve. Why, if she hadn't done a disappearing act, he . . . The thought didn't have time to get completed, before he was speaking again, his aggression dipping, but only slightly, as he questioned roughly:

'Are you saying you haven't spent this weekend with Bailey? That you haven't cut your teeth on that—amateur?'

Cut her teeth! Amateur! Suddenly it all became blindingly clear what all this was about. Croft was as mad as hell, not only because his expectations had come to nothing, but also because, having fired a semi-awakening in her, he felt cheated to think Philip had reaped the harvest.

All at once Mercy knew red-hot fury. Even while it flashed through her mind to wonder where the pre-Croft days had gone when she used to have perfectly normal conversations, she was slamming into him, her disgust evident that his mind should work that way.

'That's *it*, isn't it,' she yelled. 'That's what all this is about. You wanted me to—to cut my teeth w-with you. You were anticipating a—a weekend with me using you as a—as a—teething ring,' she spluttered in her rage. And careless that his eyes had narrowed, she slammed into him again, uncaring that she could be pricking him into retaliation. 'It was your own urges that rose up, not mine. It was *you* who needed an outlet.'

She had come to a fiery full stop, and knew it was all out in the open now. And she was too out of control to think before she spoke when, obviously stung by her disgust, by the way she was reviling him, Croft rapped back, not holding his punches:

'If at any time I ever feel the need to let my—urges, as you call them, get the better of me, it might surprise you to know that you are not the *only* female of my acquaintance.'

'Felicia Woodward,' snapped Mercy, stung in turn, jealousy turning a knife. There was nothing she could do to prevent that name from escaping.

Then she was wishing the name back. Wishing that it hadn't shot off her tongue as though it was forever to the forefront of her mind. Croft must not know what the thought of that woman could do to her, he must not.

She had lowered her eyes immediately Felicia's name was out. But in the silence that followed, she just had to look at him—and as quickly lower her eyes again.

For Croft Latimer suddenly wasn't angry any more. He was all of a sudden wearing that crooked grin which played havoc with her heart rhythm. And suddenly too, she was bracing herself for what was to come; for it had to be that he had guessed at her jealousy!

Ready to scoff at any suggestion she might be jealous, she was aware he had moved to come level with her. But when next he spoke, she saw with overwhelming relief her defences were not needed. He must have missed seeing her jealousy. Though what he did say was something she found so utterly staggering, so mind-blowing, that for several seconds she could not think straight.

'D'you know, Mercy Yeomans,' he said, with an amusement she hadn't heard in a long time, 'for a while there we sounded like an arguing married couple.' Then, humour dying, his voice deadly serious, quietly, he dropped out, 'Fancy trying it?'

Her eyes going huge in her face as she sought for comprehension, she had to look at him. 'You're suggesting . . .' she managed, but couldn't believe what he was suggesting, and could get no further. Then she heard humour in him again, as, coolly, he told her;

'I'm not suggesting anything your prim little soul could take exception to.'

Her heart was having a riot of a time within her. He

must be asking her to marry him. It was what sh
wanted above all things. And for a brief second
was touch and go whether she launched herself at hir
and said, yes, yes, yes. But that brief second clashe
with the way he had, humorously to her ear
followed up his proposal. That coolness was not wha
one would expect of a man waiting with bated breat
to hear her answer.

Her brief flash of utter rapture faded into a dee
nothingness as pride had her fighting with all she had
so that he should not know what a proper proposal fror
him, a proposal that meant something to *him*, coul
mean to her. And there was a slight thread o
amusement in her voice too, as she went to straighte
an ornament above the fireplace, and threw over he
shoulder:

'If I may borrow words from you, Croft,' she said
standing back as though to examine the alignment o
the ornament, 'you're surely not suggesting anything a
diabolical as that I should marry you, are you?'

'You wouldn't?'

'Do I look stupid?' she questioned airily, too afrai
to turn round and let him see her face in the silence tha
was building up at the back of her.

Seconds ticked by as she straightened anothe
ornament. She was scared to speak again, but sadl
wanted him to say something that would put an end t
this conversation. For she was, oh, so terribly afrai
that while it was still open, while there was still time fo
her to say yes, she might well find her unwary tongu
doing exactly that.

Then Croft was putting an end to it. Confirming fo
her that he had been in no way as serious as he had a
first seemed, because amusement was there in his voi
too when he said lightly, entirely unaffected at bein
turned down:

'You're right, of course.' Though he caused her t

ırn, anxious for him, when he added, as if to excuse what
ad just dawned on him as being a ridiculous suggestion,
t must be the pressure of work getting to me.'

She saw then what she had been too fired up to
ɔtice before. He looked as though he had slept little
cently. Obviously jet-lag had something to do with
ₐat, but he must have worked hard to get his business
ɔmpleted in under two-thirds of the time he had
łowed himself in the States.

Her heart had to rule her head then. Concern for him
ade her say gently, 'You shouldn't work so hard,
roft. Can't you let up a bit?' And, since he hadn't shot
ɛr down for offering advice he hadn't asked for, 'Can't
ɔu rest more?'

'It was in my mind to do something of the sort this
eekend.'

His reply had been tinged with mockery, as though it
ₐnused him to hear her playing mother hen. She
sregarded his mockery, she'd half expected it anyhow.
ut she paused, trying to calculate if, mockery
ccepted, Croft was telling her he would have rested
ore easily if he had known where on earth she was.
er heart jumped uselessly at the thought. But that
me empathy she had felt with him before was there at
ork again. And loving him as she did, even if she had
ɔt it wrong, and there was no time to puzzle it out
ɔw, there didn't seem to be any reason why she should
ɔld back from telling him where she had been.

'I . . .' she began. She saw she had his attention, and
ₑgan again. 'When I went away, I went to a hotel in
ₑ Cotswolds.'

'With?' he queried. But she knew from the expression
ₙ his face, the fact he wasn't getting aggressive again,
ₐt he knew she hadn't gone with Philip.

'You know full well I didn't go away with anybody,'
ₑ said, a smile in her voice, empathy still there.

His crooked grin appeared. 'I didn't want to believe

it,' he admitted, which had her idiotic heart racir
again. Then, no smile about him, seriously, he aske
'Why choose this weekend to have a weekend off?'

'Why not this weekend?' she replied, empathy beir
edged out as she prevaricated.

'You knew I was coming down.'

He had uttered his statement flatly. And she had r
answer to make. She knew that he knew the reply
that statement, just as she knew he hadn't real
believed she had gone away with Philip.

'That's why, isn't it?' he pressed, not looking tc
pleased, though not angry as he had been before. 'Yo
lit out because you knew I was coming.'

'I—had to go,' she said, wishing more than ever th
he had gone before she returned. She didn't want to te
him anything, yet she knew from the very serious tor
he was taking with her that he wouldn't be fobbed o
with less than the truth.

'Because you're afraid?' he probed.

'I'm not afraid of you.'

'I know that,' he replied shortly, then checked on th
edge of temper that had crept in. 'You're afraid c
yourself, aren't you, Mercy?' he queried, his voice quic
regretful even. 'You've lived so long in a world c
chaste kisses, you're afraid of that almighty chemist
that shakes you when we kiss.'

Not knowing what she would have said, she opene
her mouth to interrupt him; then had to be glad that I
would not let her, because what he said gave her a le
out, showing her he was no nearer to being aware th
she had gone away because of her love for him.

'That's why you went away, Mercy, because yo
thought that if I kissed you again this weekend, free
you'd be from the over-wrought emotions that held m
back before, we would both feel a return of th
chemistry. That it would ignite, get out of hand. Th
you would hate yourself for going against yo

rinciples if you gave yourself to me.'

She couldn't answer him. She guessed he would read
·om her silence confirmation of all he had said. But her
·ve for him was rising, bringing a lump to her throat
·nd tears welling to her eyes, and she couldn't speak.

Not wanting him to see how near her tears were, she
·ent to stare out of the window. He knew what he
·uld do to her, she had shown him plainly enough that
·orning when she had opened her eyes to find him in
·r room. But she just had to love him more because
·e knew that wanting her, knowing she wanted him,
·roft would not take her when her emotions were out
· gear, wouldn't try to persuade her to go against what
· saw as her principles.

Oh no, she thought, knowing he would go soon
·w, what principles she did have would not stand a
·ance if he loved her half as much as she loved him.

She was still battling against tears, when, quietly,
·s voice came again. 'I know you love it here. Be
·ppy, Mercy,' he said, with a finality that almost
·ade her turn. 'There'll be no need for you to run
·vay again.'

Mercy came away from the window and stared at the
·nt door that had just closed. She heard Croft's car
·rt up. And knew then, that although Lupin
·ottage was his property and she merely its caretaker,
· would not be coming down again—not whilst she
·s there.

Tears started to flow then. Unable to stop the flow,
·e simply sat and wept. And having done with her
·ving, that sadness still with her, she cried again when
·nlessly she left the chair she had sunk into and
·ndered into the kitchen. For there she saw the
·eque amply covering her outlay on the groceries,
·ich Croft had left.

She wiped tears from her eyes, wondering if this was
·w it was going to be. Was this all she would have of

him? His signature on a salary cheque through the p
every month. He wouldn't badger her to leave
cottage, she knew that. But he wouldn't be comi
down again. She would never see him again. Oh
she couldn't bear it. A cracked sob broke from her. S
couldn't bear not seeing him again.

When Mercy dragged herself purposelessly out of b
the next morning, there was no chink of light in
blackness of her despair. Oh, Croft, she thought, a
had him as her constant companion in whatever she
that morning.

Never was she free from that see-sawing of l
emotions. Memory was vivid in her mind of what
had said to her, what she had said to him. She tried
think it was all for the best, but common sense was
help with what she wanted and what had to be.

Reliving every word, every look, every nuance tl
had gone on yesterday, it was towards late afterno
that one memory struck and kept coming back, u
eventually it stayed and had her arguing with hers
against the hope that wanted to flicker from tl
memory.

He *had* asked her to marry him, hadn't he? Of cou
he had pleaded that pressure of work had left him
knowing what he was saying. But—but was Crof
man to ask a girl to marry him, then laugh it off a
mere slip of the tongue because he was utterly weary

Would he laugh it off, she wondered, plucking
what she knew of him, if the girl he proposed to I
rejected his proposal out of hand? Croft had his pr
too. What if he *had* been serious, she pondered,
heart going erratic at the mere thought. What if .
Her heart steadied its beat, paced down into a d
steady throb, as she remembered that he had been re;
to ask Felicia Woodward to marry him too.

That meant he wasn't truly in love with either
them. And while she couldn't be more pleased

discover that he wasn't in love with Felicia Woodward, it left her knowing that it must be desire that ruled him. And desire, she thought, wanting to be done with the hope she had found in wanting to believe he had been serious when he'd asked her to marry him, was no basis for the sort of marriage she wanted.

Marriage to Croft was impossible, she saw, still plagued by a thought that wouldn't leave. Marriage to her meant a sacred commitment. A commitment for life. The facts were plain, she was in love with Croft, he was not in love with her. And even if he had been serious in his proposal, her answer still had to be the same. She could not enter into a marriage where, once the desire it was based on had worn off, she was left wondering whether there was some other female whom he desired as he had Felicia Woodward and herself.

It wouldn't be fair to him either, she found herself thinking as night fell. How could she tie him to her by marriage when he did not love her?

And anyway, she thought an hour later, hope gone, why was she tearing herself apart? His proposal couldn't have been made in earnest. He hadn't fallen apart when she'd answered 'Do I look stupid', had he?

Loneliness of spirit had her in its grip the next day. She had gone over it all again, and was still no nearer to finding peace of mind. She tried to get down to some serious thinking about what she should do with her future, but found it impossible to concentrate. Had Croft been serious with his proposal?

By the time evening arrived she knew she couldn't carry on like this. She didn't want to marry Croft without love being there, that was a principle she had discovered, even if it was based on her fear of him wanting a divorce before the newness had gone off any wedding ring slipped over her finger. And yet, the truth was, she just couldn't take life without seeing him ever again.

Mercy sat down, and for the next half an hour gave solid, devoted attention to the thought that stirred in her as the only way open to her. There was no way she could enter into a marriage that she knew full well beforehand stood a good chance of ending up in the divorce court. She would be too unsure of her position with him to be able to build on the marriage, to try and turn his desire for her into love—a lasting love. But she was not certain that the other way wasn't just as fraught with difficulties; when she might have a chance of earning his love, a love that would endure, if, no marriage there for her to try and save, she agreed to live with him for a while.

Another half an hour went by, and at the end of that time she left her chair. She went over to the telephone and took up the receiver, her hands shaking so much she almost dropped it. Then taking a deep breath, not daring to think of her father's anger, her mother's disappointment in her, Mercy started to dial.

CHAPTER TEN

At the first two notes of the ringing tone, Mercy's hand went moist on the phone. She had made contact with his home.

Feeling a decided bundle of nerves, she gripped the instrument hard, hanging on there with a tenacity that denied that part of her that told her he was out, that she should put the phone down.

To her, the ringing tone seemed to go on for an age, the thought going through her head that maybe he was deeply involved with something in his study and wouldn't want to be disturbed. Or, maybe he wasn't in his study, came the undermining unwelcome thought, but was equally deeply involved.

Then the ringing stopped. And it was then that her jitters reached a peak, and stayed there. Croft wasn't sounding very pleased about anything as his short tones came over the wires.

'Latimer,' he said brusquely.

Her voice didn't sound like hers, she discovered when, clinging tightly to the receiver as though it were a life raft, she heard the pitch a shade higher than was usual, her words leaving her staccato, unnatural.

'I—didn't mean to—to disturb you,' she got out, in such a state she forgot to tell him who was calling and left him to guess who it was.

'Mercy!'

She swallowed, tried to answer him, but found she couldn't. Oh dear, and she'd been setting herself up to compete with the sophisticated women he knew!

'Mercy—are you all right?'

At Croft's urgent enquiry, she found her voice,

reminding herself that the sort of thing she had set her mind to, was something that was happening every day.

'Yes—yes, I'm fine,' she said.

And in the pause that followed she felt herself all of a tremble that Croft was now waiting, not unnaturally, to hear why she had telephoned him.

'Er—I rang you actually to . . .' she began, and was already floundering. 'Well,' she said, and knew that though he was making no move to hurry her, he would soon lose patience with her if she didn't spit it out. And she was saying in a rush, 'You know you asked me to marry you?' Which was not what she had meant to say at all.

To her overstrung nerves Croft's voice came back sounding oddly tense, though she was sure he wasn't tense at all when slowly he replied:

'You have thought it over? You—don't think it such a stupid idea after all?'

'No—yes—no,' she said, her mind in a quagmire. She took a calming breath, and thought she had a grip on herself. 'Well, I have been thinking, but—but . . .' She went hot and cold all over at what she had been thinking, and it was then that the grip she thought she had on herself collapsed. Her courage went and she was telling him, 'It doesn't matter,' and putting the receiver down.

An hour later she was still calling herself the biggest idiot under the sun. Other girls thought nothing of that sort of thing—look at Hilary for one.

Half an hour after that, having told herself that she wasn't like Hilary, Mercy felt calmer, but was still denigrating herself for being the biggest coward of all time. She hadn't even put her proposition to him.

It had been a stupid proposition anyway, she chided herself some time later, a ridiculous idea. On a par with playing at being married to him for a while. She went into the kitchen to make a hot drink she didn't particularly want, but which she might as well have since there seemed little point in going to bed. No point at all in going upstairs and putting out the light only to lie there wide awake stewing over what a fool Croft must think her to make a call to him and then tell him it didn't matter. She might as well stay down here for a while, she wasn't going to sleep anyway, she knew that from experience.

The water was running, so she did not hear the purr of a car. She put the electric kettle to boil, then switched it off, she didn't want a drink. There was only one thing she wanted, and she had lost that. Would never have the nerve to ring him again, she knew that too.

Alarm temporarily ousted Croft from her thoughts when she heard someone at the front door, a vision of the squatters Diane had been afraid of flashing into her mind as someone inserted a key into the lock. Her mind darted in all directions with thoughts of someone using skeleton keys to break in, while the opposing thought came, would they, when they could see a light on in the cottage?

Bravely, gulping down fear, she left the kitchen, but only to stand transfixed when she saw that the door was being pushed inwards!

Then, transfixed didn't begin to cover how she felt. Absolutely positive that he would not return to Lupin Cottage whilst she was there, she could not believe that the broad-shouldered man who had come into the room was Croft. For stunned seconds she thought that having him so constantly in her head, her mind was playing tricks on her and had conjured him up when he wasn't really there.

'Croft!' she gasped, weakly clutching the back of a chair.

'I've frightened you,' said the tall, fair-haired man

who was indeed Croft. 'I didn't mean to do that. I rather thought you might be expecting me.'

'I—no,' she stammered, her voice gone high again. 'I—Why have you come?'

There wasn't a smile about him, he hadn't been smiling before, she realised. And suddenly she was the same mass of nerves she had been when she had put the phone down, for he was saying:

'I never did much care for conversations that never got started.' And with his eyes piercing hers, quietly, he went on to ask, 'Why did you ring, Mercy?'

She spied the determined light in his eyes, and it was then that she knew he had not driven all this way at this time of night, only to be fobbed off with an 'It doesn't matter' answer.

'I . . .' she choked. 'Er—shall we sit down?'

Unhurriedly, though that determined light in his eyes did not waver, he waited until she had come round from behind her chair. Waited, not moving, until she was seated; then he took the seat that was opposite, which Mercy found, in a room that was not large, was much too close to hers.

The urge to procrastinate, to offer him some sort of refreshment, came. Over the phone she had been unable to tell him what it was all about; face to face, she found it impossible. But one hasty look at him was enough to tell her he was patiently waiting—that somehow she was going to have to tell him. The silence stretched, her nerves stretching with it. She opened her mouth, but courage failed her, and she closed it again.

'Take your time,' he instructed evenly, a threat behind his words that if it took hours for him to get it out of her, then so be it. He confirmed the threat. 'We have all night to discuss what my eyes tell me is a crisis time in your life,' he said. And then added, a gentler note there, 'You haven't slept much recently either, have you?'

That 'either' had her wondering what kept him awake at night. That was before nagging jealousy told her it was better not to know.

'Do I look such a hag?'

'You look beautiful, and you know it,' he said. But still he didn't smile, still he looked determined. And when, after another long moment of silence she had said nothing more, he was there to prompt, 'On the phone you mentioned you had been thinking over my proposal.'

'I . . .' she said, the coward in her wanting to deny she had given it any thought, the coward in her having her studying her lap. That was before some small courage came to her, courage born out of defeat. 'I have thought about it,' she said honestly, and just before her frail courage dipped, 'I've thought about it a great deal.'

'And?'

Mercy thought she heard tension in him, and flicked a glance his way, while aware it wasn't Croft who was tense, but she. She saw he was looking wholly serious, and, her hands moist, she grabbed at courage again.

'A-and—I don't think marriage is for you—not with me at any rate.'

She bit her lip and wouldn't look at him again. She knew he was a rapid thinker, was rapid in his summing up, and she would have dearly loved to know, as another long silence stretched, what he was thinking.

'You rang me to tell me that?' he queried softly.

She had been going to say so much more than that, but hope was with her that he would be satisfied that that was all her phone call had been about. She nodded her affirmative answer. And heard then that where she was too agitated to be thinking no further than the end of her nose, Croft was capable of thinking in all directions.

'Why telephone to tell me that?' he asked. 'From

what I remember of our discussion on the matter on Monday, you had already turned me down.'

Stumped, she shot a look at him and saw, still serious, he appeared to be encouraging as, softly still, he coaxed, 'Come now, Mercy, there's more to it than that, isn't there?'

Mercy stayed down for a count of ten, then, 'Yes,' she whispered. And had then to get started because the sooner it was out, she had to feel better, hadn't she? He was going to know it all anyway, everything about him said that. 'I wanted to tell you, to discuss with you the—the possibility of . . .' she dried up.

Then she found that Croft had pulled his chair round to an angle to the side of hers. He was there beside her, not touching, but leaning forward and looking into her face, though she wouldn't look at him as he prompted:

'What possibility is this, my dear? This possibility that brings a blush to your cheeks?'

That 'my dear' gently spoken, had her half turning, her eyes flicking to him and away, her fingers picking at the piping on her chair.

'I can't marry you because . . . I can't marry you—I'm not even sure you seriously meant it when you asked me, anyway. But . . .'

She knew she was going to tell him now, but she paused, needing to gain her second wind. And was out in a wilderness on her own, for he wasn't prompting her any more, but sat unmoving, waiting to hear what else she had to say.

'But,' she resumed, the moment arriving to tell him, 'b-but I rang to tell you I will—l-live with you for a while—if you l-like.'

Her colour was crimson as she came to an end. No power on earth would have made her look at him to see his reaction. But thinking she had put it fairly clearly, for all her stammering to get it out, she was entirely unprepared for the question that came from him, a thread of strain in his voice, she thought, as he asked:

'You are saying you will not marry me, but that you will live with me as though we were married?'

She nodded, her vocal cords gone into hiding at the overwhelming embarrassment that she had, coldly it seemed to her, offered herself to him.

'Have I got this right?' he stressed, sounding to her as if he found what she had just said unbelievable. And doing nothing to dispel her embarrassment, 'You are saying you are prepared to come to me without marriage. That you are prepared to be my friend, my helpmate, my companion?'

Not looking at him, again she nodded. And heard then, disbelief still there in his voice, an added note she couldn't quite pin-point there too but which somehow sounded as though he was holding himself in check, the taut way in which he continued his questioning.

'You understand that to live with me would encompass your sharing my bed?' he asked. 'You would include sharing my bed in your offer, would you, Mercy?'

He was making very sure she knew what she was offering, she thought. But she had gone too far to deny now that her offer had been total.

'Yes,' she said, 'I understand that.'

Croft did not immediately make any reply. And, unable to look at him, it was in those moments of motionless silence that she began to suffer the agony of suspecting that to have what she was offering handed to him on a plate, had merely turned him off her.

But she was to suffer the most searing of all agony when he moved suddenly from being stock still, and with one hand taking charge of her hand picking at her chair, his other hand came to turn her face to him. And very quietly, his grey eyes pinning hers, he then said:

'For how long, Mercy, have you known yourself in love with me?'

Instantly she lowered her eyes. Denial poured from her. 'I'm not in love with you, I'm not,' she refuted, snatching at what she could in the way of protection.

Too late she saw that he was too smart for her. She saw too late that he had looked straight through her offer to live with him. That had been the reason for his disbelief, she comprehended at last. It wasn't at all what she had been thinking, that he was astounded she should make the offer in the first place.

'It's just—just that it's—lonely here sometimes,' she said, lying desperately, ready to lie her head off in her need to find an alternative excuse.

She flicked the briefest of glances at him, hoping to see he had accepted her lie as the truth—and caught the first signs of his crooked grin. And it was then that she knew Croft was a man whose intelligence it wouldn't do to under-rate. He knew she was lying!

'But you love the solitude, I know you do,' he said quietly. 'You told me yourself that you did.'

'Well—well . . .' she struggled. She hadn't a leg to stand on and she knew it. And all she wanted then was for him to go and leave her to lick her wounded pride in private. 'Forget I said anything,' she said huskily. 'Forget you came here tonight. It—it was a mistake.'

But he was shaking his head as if to say 'No way' before she had half finished. 'Like hell I will,' he said. He was making her succumb by revealing what he knew of her, and what his intelligence had brought him. 'I've learned a lot about you in the short time I've known you. To suggest you live with me is not something you would do lightly. Proof of that is in the shadows beneath your eyes—those shadows that tell of wakeful nights.'

'Everybody has a bad night once in a while,' she said, trying to find some spirit.

'You're not the sort to hop in and out of bed with anybody,' he said, as though he hadn't heard her. 'You don't sleep around. It would be a mammoth decision for you. A decision you wouldn't tear yourself apart with unless you cared deeply for the man you decided finally you could live with.'

And while she was going under for the third time though still trying in vain to prevent him from being sure that she was, as he had said, in love with him, she heard a hint of aggression when he went on to tell her:

'Don't try to tell me you have just offered yourself to me solely to assuage the loneliness of your life here. It really won't wash.'

'Everyone gets lonely sometimes,' she persevered, hanging on, not wanting her pride in the dust.

'To the extent of that commitment? Not you, girl,' he said shortly. 'You want me as I want you.'

For a moment her heart set off at a sprint. Only for fresh dejection to set in that he meant that word 'want' in only the physical sense.

'There's more to living with someone besides sex,' she said, unguarded in her blunt rebuttal of what she thought he meant.

'Agreed,' he said. 'Though I hope you don't intend to deny, too, that you have wanted me in the same way I have wanted you.'

She didn't answer. He knew the answer anyway, she thought, remembering those clinging moments when she would have been his had he not let out the truth.

'But it's more than that,' he went on, seeming not to need her reply, and making her heartbeats erratic again. 'Deny it if you must, but you feel something for me, Mercy. Why else are you jealous of Felicia Woodward? Jealousy was there in your voice on Monday when . . .'

'No!' she said, turning her head from him.

'That's what I thought when later I had to discount what my ears had told me,' he said. Then with a gentle but firm hand, he turned her head so she should look at him, a warmth in his eyes as he revealed, 'It was a jealousy I was delighted to hear at the time.'

'You were?' She had no idea why he should be delighted, but something in his look was telling her it wasn't because of any previously unseen sadistic streak.

'Well,' he said, 'I have suffered enough jealousy over that jackass Bailey to know jealousy when I hear it.'

'You've been jealous over Philip!' Her heart leapt, then went tumbling, to hear him say:

'I spent last weekend in torment telling myself you couldn't be with him, yet not being able to shake off the notion.'

Oh, how foolish her heart was, she thought sadly. For all of a few seconds she had let herself believe he had been jealous because he cared for her. But it wasn't that. She remembered his comment about her cutting her teeth, and knew then there was a possessive streak in him. It wasn't jealousy he had felt, she was sure, purely wounded male pride that she might be with Philip as he thought she should have been with him.

'You think it was jealousy because you didn't want me to be with Philip?' she questioned, trying to raise her voice above the flatness that was in her.

'I don't know what else you'd call it, when I wanted to find you wherever you were. Find you and tear him limb from limb.' A smile broke from him then. 'You too,' he confessed, 'for all the regard I have for you.'

'The regard you have—for me!' she echoed, her ridiculous heart not knowing how to behave, as hope started to spiral upward again.

'The same—regard—I discovered I had for you that morning I arrived early and stood at the foot of your bed. You lay there asleep, one of your arms across the pillow, nothing in you but innocence.'

His voice had grown warm to match the look in his eyes. And it was all she could do to stop herself from

gulping at that warm look. Croft had said he had some
regard for her. Did that warm look mean he cared? She
was too scared of a let-down to risk finding out.

'I saw you. Wanted to lie with you,' he said softly.
'Wanted to hold you in my arms, wanted to hold you close.'

'To—make love to me?' The ridiculous thought that
he might be meaning his regard was more than just
physical, was already being spirited away, only to come
tiptoeing back, when he replied:

'No, my dear. Not then. I wanted to protect that
innocence, not take it. I wanted to protect you. To lie
quiet beside you. Not even to talk.'

For countless moments she basked in the beauty of
his words. She felt the prick of tears at the sensitivity in
him that hadn't wanted to harm her then. And was lost
as she pictured how it had been. Then she remembered
what had happened when she had awakened.

'But you did—did—would have taken ... If you
hadn't slipped up and told me ...'

'I didn't slip up,' he denied. 'I'd been intrigued by
you since the moment I first saw you. But after the way
you'd tried to make me believe you fancied me, I
thought you in turn deserved to believe what I had led
you to think. And I'll admit there was no thought in me
to tell you differently when I took you in my arms and
felt you responding, eager to learn anything I would
teach you,' his hand came to whisper a caress to her
cheek, to smooth at the blush that had flared. 'But at
the last moment, when had I not said anything you
would have been mine, I found I couldn't let you find
out the truth for yourself.'

Her cheeks hot, she didn't know which of the trails
he had led her down to take up first. 'You've been
intrigued by me since Hilary's wedding?' she managed
to get out. If she was going to be in despair when he
had gone, though punishing herself as it might be, then
she had to know more.

'As you know, I had only one aim in mind when I went to that wedding,' he reminded her. 'As I anticipated there was nothing dewy-eyed about the bride, who looked as hard as nails as she rushed down the aisle to her pot of gold, and the bridesmaid behind her had a look in her eyes that said she was like minded. And then I saw you. Fresh, different from the rest, and I couldn't figure where you fitted in.'

'I saw you looking at me,' she murmured, a glow in her heart that wouldn't listen to common sense.

'I couldn't take my eyes off you,' he admitted. 'I was still wondering what the devil you were doing mixed up with that eye-to-the-main-chance bunch, when the photographer got busy. I was still around, which hadn't been my intention at all, when your friend went into her routine about "I must have my photograph taken with each bridesmaid".'

'You didn't intend staying around for the photographs?'

'My only intention was to witness the event, then to get to the nearest phone box to let Diane know the field was clear if she wanted it.'

'But—but that—that means you had no intention of going to the reception,' she gasped.

'Would I deny the most lovely of the bridesmaids when she came looking for a lift?' he asked, that irresistible quirk of amusement she was hooked on showing itself at her amazement.

'But none of this would have started if I hadn't . . .'

'It wouldn't,' he agreed, his face serious once more. 'But it did get started, and I hope I'm not going to be sorry I went with you to that reception.'

That Croft had said he hoped he wasn't going to be sorry, was enough to fuel her heart into another energetic outburst. Then it was abruptly sent plummeting as she had to remember that it wasn't because of her that he had gone to the reception.

'You came with me because you'd guessed Hilary was
ar to passing out with fright,' she said flatly.

'That's what I kept telling myself—that I was only
ere to make you both sweat it out,' he replied. And
vned, 'I knew it wasn't in my mind to have a word
ith Giles Norman even before I saw how vulnerable
looked, so I had to give myself some reason for
ing there. I kept telling myself I was only there
cause I didn't like being played for a sucker. But,' his
in was wry as he confessed, 'you'd got to me, Mercy.
uch as I didn't want to believe it and called myself a
w names when in your flat, on the point of leaving
u to sleep it off, I discovered I couldn't go out
rough the door and leave you to cope on your own if
u awoke ill.'

She had to believe that. It was similar to what he
d told her before. But even though her heart was
joicing that she had 'got to him' and that could
ean anything, or, her spirits dipped, nothing, she
as questioning:

'It was because you knew I had played—tried to play
u for a sucker, that, that you let me think we—had—
hen I woke up and found myself in bed with you?'

'Your face was a picture when you saw me there,' he
id. 'I doubt I would have resisted the urge to *play you
ong* for a few minutes, with or without your
volvement in Hilary Driver's schemes.'

'But it went on longer than a few minutes,' she
inted out.

'Bailey arrived,' Croft said. 'I discovered you were
gaged to him,' and he admitted, 'I discovered I wasn't
ppy with the knowledge. It was then I told myself
at because of your little plot to keep me out of the
ay, you didn't deserve that I should tell you I hadn't
uched you.'

'But that wasn't the real reason?'

Croft looked deeply into her eyes, the grey in his

warm, gentle. Mercy held her breath. They look
loving too.

'Oh, Mercy mine,' he breathed. 'Don't you know
the reason? Haven't you yet seen what I've been tell
you ever since I came in?'

Dumbly she shook her head. Oh, how she wanted
believe what she thought she saw in his eyes. But
couldn't be. It just couldn't be. Just as she knew s
would be making herself the biggest fool of all time,
she dared to believe it.

He let go her hand, his hands going to take hold
her shoulders in a firm, steady grip. Then, when s
wasn't looking away, his eyes fixed on hers, he told h

'You have made me an offer I know it has taken a
for you to make. But, my dearest love, I am afraid it
an offer I cannot accept.'

'Oh,' said Mercy, who thought she had known
about confusion, and then some. But who right at th
moment was having the greatest of difficulty
connecting the fact she had been turned down, with th
love-look in his eyes, and the fact he had just called h
his dearest love.

'But, my dear,' he went on tenderly, which was
help at all in getting her through her mass of confusi
'I hope with all my heart you will accept the offer
made to you.'

'The offer you . . .' was as far as she got, wh
hurtling through came understanding that he must
talking of his marriage proposal which she had alrea
turned down.

'Will you marry me, my darling?' he asked, nothi
but sincerity in the eyes holding hers.

'I . . .' was all she could manage. Her heart w
racing. He *had* been serious before, it *had* been his pri
at her rejection that had made him make light of it.

And then he was having her heart ready to le
straight out of her body. For his hands gripped her w

an intensity that was near to being painful at the time she took in answering him, and Croft, a man she had never thought to see plead, was saying:

'You've got to marry me. You've got to be in love with me, I can't have made a mistake. You know I love you, you've got to know that . . .'

'You—love me?' she whispered, tears spurting to her eyes. 'You love me?'

'My darling, haven't I been telling you so this past half hour?'

'Oh, Croft,' was all she was able to say. And the next moment, those hands on her shoulders were drawing her to her feet, the better for him to hold her close to him, close up to his heart.

'Darling, darling, darling,' he said hoarsely. And was content for long heart-thundering minutes to hold her like that, to hold her close as though he would never let her go.

Then he had a need to look into her face, to see there the love in her eyes; still having to hear her say what he wanted to hear, though she was holding nothing back.

'You do love me, Mercy?' he questioned. And she could see a definite tension in him as he waited for her answer.

'Oh yes,' she cried. 'Oh yes, I love you, Croft. Never have I felt this depth of feeling before.'

'My love,' he said thickly, and her confession that she had not loved Philip Bailey as she loved him, made him pull her closer. His need to kiss her then became too much and he rained tiny adoring kisses on her face, before at last he claimed her mouth in a kiss that brought her arms round him, and threatened to have her senseless as willingly she kissed him back.

'My beloved darling,' he said tenderly, breaking his kiss and content for a while just to look and look at her.

Then he was asking the question that she had lashed

herself too long and grievingly over for that grief to be
forgotten. Had lacerated herself with too much pain for
those same painful heart-searing mutilations not to be
remembered.

'And you will marry me?'

Tears came to her eyes then. A sadness in her look
that told him something was wrong, badly wrong. And
there was a touch of desperation in him as he shook her
slightly in his anxiety.

'What is it? What's wrong? Mercy, for heaven's sake
You're going to marry me, aren't you? You're in love with
me as I'm in love with you. You've got to marry me!'

It would have been so easy to be persuaded. But even
loving him as she did, she respected marriage too much
to enter into it with any doubt that it would last.
Feeling her heart was splintering inside her, her arms
came from around him. Gently her sensitive fingers
touched his face.

'Oh, my darling, I love you so,' was wrenched from
her as tears spilled from her eyes and down her cheeks.
Her voice breaking as she made herself go on. 'But—
but I cannot—marry you.'

A hush seemed to fall upon the room. The word,
'Cannot?' coming from Croft in a hoarse gust of breath.
His look at her tear-wet face was stunned, incredulous,
as his hand came up as though it was second nature for
him to try to ease her sorrow.

And then that hand fell away before it could touch
her, and regardless that she was distressed, in tears,
aggression was breaking in him, exploding with the
words:

'Why? Why can't you marry me? What the hell are
you playing at? You're going to marry me my girl,
you're mine. Make no mistake about that.'

'Croft, darling, please,' Mercy tried—then found she
was being pushed down into a chair, Croft standing
threateningly over her, as he demanded:

'Out with it. And if you're playing me for a fool, if you're two-timing me with . . .'

That he was still crazily jealous of Philip was there in his eyes. Knowing the torture of jealousy, she interrupted him with the only thing she could think of to ease the pain of that torture.

'I'm in love with you, Croft,' she said quietly, 'and with you only.' She saw it was all she needed to say to take the heat, the aggression out of him.

But he was still looking stunned when he straightened from his threatening stance. She saw him swallow, then suck in his cheeks as he got himself under control. He moved a chair to come and sit directly in front of her, his hands coming out to take hold of hers. Then quietly, slowly, his jaw working, he looked at her, and said:

'The love I have for you, Mercy Yeomans, will surmount any obstacle. If you have some dark secret in your cupboard you haven't told me about, then I'd like to hear about it so we can beat it to a pulp together.'

Sadly she smiled. 'There's no dark secret,' she said softly. 'Just a belief in me that marriage, for me at any rate, has to be for all time.'

'On the matter of our marriage, your views coincide with mine,' he said, his eyes never leaving her face, his tone as serious as hers. 'So where's the problem?'

'You say you love me, and—and I think you do—now.' She wanted to look away when she came to the next bit, but just by being Croft he was making her look at him when she said, 'But, not too long ago you were in love with Felicia Woodward. Were going to . . .' her voice faltered, as with the suddenness of lightning in a storm, the darkness of his brow cleared. Though whatever had come to him to say, he waited until she had ended, 'Only recently, you were going to ask her to marry you too. I c-couldn't bear it if you soon fell out of love with me, and in love with somebody else.'

The moment she had finished, before her words had

faded, Croft answered. 'My jealous, beautiful darling,' he said, a smile curving his mouth. 'Aside from the fact I could have the same nightmares that up until recently you yourself were planning to marry someone else,' he paused, seeing in her eyes that she had never taken that into her consideration—that it had jolted her, 'I think now is as good a time as any to tell you,' he paused again, a wicked devilment in his eyes, 'that not for one single·moment did I ever consider asking Felicia Woodward to be my wife.'

'But you said . . .' she gasped.

'Forget what I said then, and believe me now,' he bade her, raising both her hands to his lips, kissing first one and then the other. 'If I remember correctly,' he said, with the air of a man who hadn't forgotten a thing, 'I told you that morning, when you awoke and found me there, that you had ruined any chance of my becoming engaged to her.'

'That's right, you did,' said Mercy, having had ample time since Monday to remember with clarity every deed, word, act, every when, every where.

'Only minutes before I had discovered the depth of my feeling for you.'

'That you were in love with me?'

He nodded. 'What was a mere male to do, Mercy?' he asked. 'I knew you weren't in love with me. For the first time in my life I knew uncertainty. Uncertainty brought on by this colossal thing that had happened to me. I was scared, my darling, scared of making a fool of myself, and my fear spurred me to invent a cover-up.'

'Oh,' she said, stunned herself. Joy filtered into her heart, turning the torturing days and nights she had spent into nothing. 'But,' she said, still a shadow of pale green lurking, 'you were fond of her?' And nothing was wrong with her memory either. 'She was in your home that first time I telephoned. It was she who answered the phone.'

'That she calmly answered my phone when I was at hand and then demanded to know from you who was calling, was the least of her taking ways,' he told her. 'She went out of my mind the moment I heard your voice. I forgot she was even in the apartment.'

Mercy's pleased smile just had to peep out at that admission, though it was followed by a small wrinkle on her brow, that immediately had him asking:

'What is it, sweetheart? Let's get it all out of the way now. I want that nothing shall disturb you.'

'It was *I* who contacted you,' she revealed her thoughts. 'If I hadn't phoned that night, I might never have seen you again.'

'Don't you believe it,' he was quick to tell her. 'I took the magnetism of you back with me to London, my love. Fought against the pull of you, I admit, by not waiting around when I came down here to leave you a key. But I still hadn't told you what had *not* happened that night, so I knew that if necessary I had an excuse to contact you.'

'But with me as your caretaker you didn't need an excuse to come and see me,' she said innocently, and saw in the wicked grin he sent her, that that was exactly why she was his caretaker, the job another of his inventions. 'You rogue,' she said, but she had to smile.

'Going to forgive me, darling?' he asked, not looking the least tiny bit sorry, seeing he was forgiven before he went on, 'I had cause to be grateful to Felicia Woodward. She presented me with another excuse to come down to see you.'

'Because of what I'd told her when she came to see me?'

Croft nodded, and continued, 'When I finished sorting her out for taking it on herself to seek out my retreat and its occupant—happily,' he paused to insert, sending the last of her jealousy on its way, 'that was the last time I saw her. I then thought I had better come and ask a few questions on why you had told her what you had, when you had no memory if I had so much as kissed you.'

'I shall never forget that first kiss,' she whispered.

'Nor I,' he agreed. 'Nor that magical moment we shared just before I left for the States,' he said, showing her he had thought that parting kiss as beautiful as she had done. 'I was hard put to tear myself away after that,' he confessed.

'I never guessed,' said Mercy, and recalled then she had never really found out why he had come that weekend before he went away, anyway. 'Why did you come then?' she asked.

'Because I had to,' he said simply. 'I knew myself in love with you. Knew I was committed to the States trip. But I couldn't face not seeing you again for what could have been another three weeks.'

Joy burst from its barrier at his words. Croft loved her, she now knew he did. Loved her with a love that was enduring, lasting. She smiled because she couldn't help it, happiness was in her grasp.

'You must have worked hard to get your business completed in under two weeks,' she said softly.

'I worked like a maniac to get back to you,' he said tenderly. 'Had to phone you as soon after I had landed as I could, simply because I was aching to hear your voice. Then I had to cover up again by dreaming up an excuse for calling, inventing a mundane grocery list. Then went quietly insane with jealousy when you said you were leaving. I thought Bailey must have got to you in my absence.' He broke off, his face almost stern as he said, 'You are never going to talk of leaving me again, are you, Mercy? I swear my heart could never take another shock like that.'

She shook her head and saw a magical smile beam over his features. Then as she watched she saw his face suddenly straighten in solemn lines. Watched and saw him sit back in his chair. And then heard his voice deep, gravelly, as he asked:

'Are you going to come over here and tell you you'll marry me, Mercy Yeomans?'

Mercy heard that thread of anxiety in his voice, and at once she stood up. But she stood for only a second. Then as she saw Croft's arms open wide to receive her, some inner propulsion sent her quickly on to his lap and into those arms. Arms that closed round her and held her fiercely as though to say there was no way he was going to let her go now.

'Oh, Croft Latimer, I love you,' she cried. 'Just say when!'

A GRACIOUS ENGLISH TRADITION

Tea is "the sweetest dew of Heaven." So declared Lu Yü, a great Chinese connoisseur of the brew, more than a thousand years ago. Through the centuries, millions of people have agreed with him. It was primarily for tea that the European sailing clippers opened the route to China in the 1660s. In its early years in England tea was considered so valuable that it was sometimes sold in jewelry shops.

The English—and, incidentally, the Dutch and the Russians—took to tea as though they had been waiting for its advent all their lives. Samuel Pepys noted his first taste of "tee" in his famous diary in September 1660. Alexander Pope and other well-known poets gave it honorable mention in their writing. The amount of tea imported into the British Isles jumped from 143 pounds in 1669 to 63 million pounds in 1869.

Oddly enough, the English tradition of afternoon tea didn't begin until about 1840 when Anna Marie, Duchess of Bedford, popularized the custom—mainly because her family had shipping interests in tea!

But in spite of this leafy shrub's firm adoption by the West and its cultivation in such countries as India and Ceylon, the homeland of tea remains indisputably China. One or other of the two most common Chinese words for the drink, *ch'a* and *tay,* have gone into practically every language, from Russian and French to Swahili. In English both forms exist; in the British Isles the phrase "cuppa char" is as familiar as "cuppa tea."

We are sure Lu Yü would have been pleased at the worldwide acceptance of his favorite drink!

ROBERTA LEIGH

A specially designed collection of six exciting love stories by one of the world's favorite romance writers—Roberta Leigh, author of more than 60 bestselling novels!

1 Love in Store
2 Night of Love
3 Flower of the Desert
4 The Savage Aristocrat
5 The Facts of Love
6 Too Young to Love

Available now wherever paperback books are sold, or available through Harlequin Reader Service. Simply complete and mail the coupon below.

Harlequin Reader Service

In the U.S.
P.O. Box 52040
Phoenix, AZ 85072-9988

In Canada
649 Ontario Street
Stratford, Ontario N5A 6W2

Please send me the following editions of the Harlequin Roberta Leigh Collector's Editions. I am enclosing my check or money order for $1.95 for each copy ordered, plus 75¢ to cover postage and handling.

☐ 1   ☐ 2   ☐ 3   ☐ 4   ☐ 5   ☐ 6

Number of books checked_____ @ $1.95 each = $_____
N.Y. state and Ariz. residents add appropriate sales tax $_____
Postage and handling $____.75____
                                              TOTAL $_____

I enclose_____

(Please send check or money order. We cannot be responsible for cash sent through the mail.) Price subject to change without notice.

NAME_____
                    (Please Print)
ADDRESS_____ APT. NO._____

CITY_____

STATE/PROV._____ ZIP/POSTAL CODE_____

Offer expires February 29, 1984   30856000000

RL-N